"What did you say?"

His hands were thrust into the pockets of his jeans, the shrug he gave her completely dismissive. "We aren't getting divorced in September," he told her dryly.

He had said that! But he couldn't be serious. This had to be his warped idea of a joke.

The same way she had thought Emily and Greg's engagement announcement was a joke...?

But that was different. Their children weren't married yet, and they never would be if she had her way. She had served her time; two years as Zack's wife was long enough for anybody—even if they hadn't shared the same home!

His mocking voice followed her. "After last night, divorce between us is out of the question...."

CAROLE MORTIMER is the author of more than eighty top-selling romance novels. Her strong traditional stories with their distinctly modern appeal, fascinating characters and involving plots have earned her an enthusiastic audience worldwide. Carole Mortimer lives on the Isle of Man with her family and a menagerie of pets. She claims this busy household has helped to inspire her writing.

Books by Carole Mortimer

HARLEQUIN PRESENTS PLUS

HARLEQUIN PRESENTS

Carole Mortimer

MOTHER
— OF THE —
BRIDE

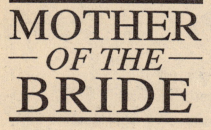

Harlequin Books

TORONTO • NEW YORK • LONDON
AMSTERDAM • PARIS • SYDNEY • HAMBURG
STOCKHOLM • ATHENS • TOKYO • MILAN
MADRID • WARSAW • BUDAPEST • AUCKLAND

Frank,
As always, with love.

ISBN 0-373-11607-1

MOTHER OF THE BRIDE

CHAPTER ONE

Mr G. Neilson
and Miss E. Palmer.
The engagement is joyfully announced
between Gregory, son of Mr Z. Neilson,
of Knightsbridge, London, and Emily,
daughter of Mrs H. Palmer, of London,
W14.

HELEN choked on a mouthful of orange juice
as the announcement in *The Times* almost
seemed to leap out of the page at her. Emily
and Greg? What on earth——? This had to be
some sort of practical joke! There was no
way——

'What is it, Helen?' The man seated across
the breakfast table frowned at her enquiringly.

She immediately folded the newspaper, announcement inwards, deliberately keeping her
movements unhurried, mopping up the orange juice she had spilt in her initial reaction,

with the snowy white napkin from her knee, smiling reassuringly at her father.

'The juice went the wrong way,' she dismissed lightly. Her father had a heart condition and she didn't want him upset by what was, after all, just a practical joke being carried out on Emily by one of her friends because it was her birthday today. Except that Helen's father would find it no funnier than Helen did herself.

'It was very clumsy of you, Helen.' He stood up to get a damp cloth.

She felt irritated at the rebuke. 'It's only juice, and the tablecloth will wash,' she snapped—and then wished she hadn't as her father looked at her with hurt reproach for her uncharacteristic sharpness.

But that announcement in the newspaper had shaken her, she had to admit, for all that she knew it was nonsense.

'I'm sorry,' she sighed, standing up too. 'I'll have to go, I have three weddings on today.' Nevertheless, she automatically began to clear the breakfast things from the table before she went, with the economy of movement that was typical of her.

'Leave that, Helen,' her father chided. 'I can do it when you've gone.'

She smiled at him affectionately for the offer, completing the task, feeling slightly guilty for her earlier abruptness. 'Don't forget we're meeting Emily for dinner tonight,' she reminded him as she pulled on the jacket to her black tailored suit, the high-necked light blue blouse she wore beneath making the grey of her eyes look almost the same colour.

He looked offended at the implication that he was becoming absent-minded, loath to admit even to himself that he was seventy-eight. 'As if I would forget my granddaughter's eighteenth birthday!'

As if any of them *could*, Helen smiled inwardly; Emily had been driving them all mad with it for weeks now!

Tonight they were having an intimate dinner for the three of them; tomorrow Emily was having a party at a local hotel for all her friends. It had been their way of including her grandfather in the celebrations without putting him through the ordeal of a large, noisy party.

Helen paused to look at her reflection in the hall mirror on her way to the front door, not with any feelings of vanity in mind; it was an everyday habit that she had to check her appearance before she left for the florist's shop she ran in town.

Short dark hair showed no signs of greying, wide grey eyes surrounded by long dark lashes, her nose small and slightly snub, adding to the impression of youth, her mouth wide and smiling, her complexion smooth and creamy. She had had more than her fair share of troubles over the years, and yet none of that showed in the gamine beauty of her face.

It didn't even occur to her that she didn't look old enough to be the mother of an eighteen-year-old daughter, that she had in fact been younger than Emily was today when she had given birth to her lovely scatter-brained daughter; at thirty-five she only looked old enough to be Emily's older sister.

'See you this evening,' she called out to her father as, neatness checked, she carried on to the door, her thoughts already turning to the floral displays and bouquets she had to get ready for the weddings today. Luckily they were all afternoon weddings, otherwise she would have had to be in to the shop at six this morning rather than eight-thirty. She would then have been like a wet rag for Emily's dinner party tonight!

It wasn't until she was unlocking her silver-coloured Metro, which helped her get through the London traffic so well, that she realised she had brought the folded newspaper out with her. It had been done subconsciously, but thank God she hadn't left it in the house for her father to find and read!

She waited until she had got in behind the wheel of the car before looking at the announcement once more herself.

There was no mistake, she realised heavily, as she read it carefully once again. It *was* Emily and Greg. And Greg meant Zack... She wondered if he had seen the announcement yet; *The Times* had always been his morning newspaper.

Well, practical joke or not, there would have to be a retraction put in as quickly as possible!

And she would have to ring Emily as soon as she got to the shop, warn her of what had happened. No doubt her bubbly daughter would find the whole thing hilarious. And if it had been anyone other than Greg *Neilson* perhaps Helen might have found it amusing too.

Her full-time assistant, Sonia, and the two young girls who usually helped out on a Saturday were already waiting outside the shop to be let in when Helen parked her car on the road opposite just before eight-thirty, getting out and taking the newspaper with her. Thank God none of the three girls waiting for her read *The Times*, although she realised there would probably be some explaining to do to some friends today who would wonder if the announcement was correct, and why they hadn't been told sooner.

As it very often was first thing in the morning, the telephone was ringing inside the shop as she unlocked the door for them all to enter, the two younger girls making a start on taking out the buckets of blooms and arranging them on the pavement outside; by nine o'clock the shop would be ready to open. Sonia went straight through to the back of the shop to make a start on making up the bouquets from the boxes of fresh flowers that had already been delivered.

Helen opened the order book that always lay beside the telephone, picking up the pen next to it before lifting the receiver, knowing it would probably be some poor man who had forgotten his wife's birthday or their wedding anniversary and wanted to know if it was too late to get flowers delivered today; these frantic early-morning calls were invariably from such worried men. Helen always felt sorry for them.

'Palmer Florists, can I help you?' She smiled as she answered the call; Sonia would make the delivery later on today, and the wife in question would never even guess at her husband's frantic early-morning call to the florist.

'Helen.'

Just that. But it was more than enough.

Her hand tightened about the receiver until her knuckles showed white, but she replied smoothly, 'Zack.'

'You've seen the newspaper?' Again he spoke with the minimum of effort needed to make himself understood. Again it was enough.

Two could play at that game! 'Yes,' Helen answered as economically.

'I think we should talk, don't you?' It was an instruction, not a request.

It had always been so with this man; he ordered, everyone else jumped to obey.

Helen stiffened resentfully. 'I don't see any point——'

'Our children have seen fit to announce their engagement to each other—unless *you* put it in?' The idea suddenly seemed to occur to him.

'Certainly not,' she snapped.

'I didn't think so,' he rasped. 'In that case, the announcement seems more than enough reason to me for the two of *us* to talk!'

She felt the colour burn her cheeks at the intended rebuke. Ridiculous. The whole thing was a practical joke anyway, so why should she feel guilty for refusing to discuss it with this man? Because that was exactly what he was trying to make her feel.

'It's a joke, Zack,' she told him impatiently. On all of us, she thought wearily. Whoever the little devils were who had done this, they couldn't realise just how much of a joke it was!

'What the hell makes you think that?' he bit out tautly.

She stiffened. 'I think I have a close enough relationship with Emily for her to have told me about something like this,' she scorned.

'Do you?' Zack returned softly.

She gave an outraged gasp. 'Now look here——'

'I'll call at the shop at four o'clock this afternoon,' he cut in arrogantly.

That had always been the trouble with Zack; he moved too fast for her, too fast for most people! 'I don't——'

'We can talk then,' he spoke autocratically over her objection.

'—have the time to see you this afternoon,' she finished determinedly—and then realised how aggressive she had probably sounded as there was a pointed silence on the other end of the line. Well, damn it, he wasn't even letting her finish what she wanted to say! She drew in a controlling breath. 'It's Saturday, Zack,' she reminded him evenly. 'I have three weddings today, and——'

'And our children have just announced a fourth!' he bit out tautly. 'That is more important than anything else *either* of us has to do today.' He was reminding her that, as a surgeon, he was probably busier than she was!

'I'll be at the shop at four,' he repeated firmly before replacing the receiver with a decisive click.

Helen's hand was shaking so much—whether just from anger at being bullied in this way, or from the shock of having to talk to him at all, she wasn't sure!—that it took her three flustered attempts to replace her own receiver.

One thing she was sure of: Zack would be here, as stated, at four o'clock this afternoon! He was a man who always did exactly what he said he was going to do, no matter how unpleasant the task—and she certainly had no reason to believe, if it weren't for Emily and Greg, that he was any more eager to talk to her than she was to him. The opposite, in fact!

Sonia wandered into the tiny room they laughingly called the office at that moment, her preoccupied expression telling Helen that she was looking for the list of today's orders. But her expression turned to one of concern as she glanced up and saw how pale Helen was. 'All right?'

All right? All right? No, it was not *all right*; just talking to Zack Neilson had totally unnerved her.

'Fine,' she answered shakily, wishing she sounded more convincing. 'I just—I have a phone call to make, and I'll be right with you.'

Sonia, a ravishing blonde in her early twenties, wasn't fooled for a minute by Helen's attempt at a smile. But over the two years the two of them had worked together they had learnt to respect each other's privacy. And so, with one last concerned glance, Sonia disappeared with today's list of deliveries.

Helen quickly picked up the receiver and dialled Emily's number, well aware that time was marching on, and she still had those three weddings this afternoon.

The telephone rang and rang at the other end, and when a sleepy voice did eventually answer she knew instantly that it wasn't Emily's. There was a further delay while the still-sleepy flatmate, one of the three girls Emily shared with, wandered off to get Emily from her bedroom. Only to finally wander back again minutes later to inform Helen that

Emily wasn't in her room and that she must have gone down to the library early to study.

Helen knew it was much more likely that Emily had been to an all-night party and hadn't even got home yet; the library wasn't even open for another ten minutes!

Emily was at college studying English Literature, but as she was able to breeze through any studying involved with ease she tended to have a fairly hectic social life. God knew what the party tomorrow night was going to turn out like!

Helen thanked the flatmate and rang off. She would have to try to catch up with Emily later on in the day. Anyway, if she knew her daughter, Emily would wonder what all the fuss was about a silly practical joke. And she wouldn't have too much sympathy with Helen's agitation at Zack's involvement; Emily had always found him absolutely charming. She hadn't known him in the same way Helen had!

The morning passed in a rush as she and Sonia dealt with all the flowers for the afternoon, Sonia taking the van to deliver the flowers to the appropriate churches before carrying on with their other deliveries, Helen

taking the bouquets, corsages, and button-
holes to the homes of the brides herself. After
weeks of deliberation over colours and arrangements, she then felt it was totally unfair
to present the nervous bride with a complete
stranger delivering the flowers on the actual
wedding day.

That June afternoon Helen saw a young
bride who had obviously come to the decision that 'if it didn't work out there was always divorce', a second bride who was calmly
serene about the whole thing—mainly because of the half-bottle of cooking sherry she
and her mother had shared during the morning!—and the third bride who couldn't stop
crying because she was sure she was doing the
wrong thing and it was too late to call it all
off.

By the time Helen drove back to the shop at
five minutes to four she felt like joining her!

It hadn't been an easy day by any means,
and Zack's expected arrival in five minutes
didn't help one little bit. It would be too much
to hope that he had telephoned while she had
been out and cancelled the meeting.

'Any calls?' she prompted Sonia hopefully, putting the kettle on for a much-needed

cup of tea; the homes of the brides were usually much too chaotic for them to even think of offering the long-suffering florist refreshment!

'Business,' Sonia shrugged. 'And a few friends who said they would call you back at home over the weekend,' she dismissed easily, having no idea why Helen's flustered expression suddenly took on a hunted look.

But Helen knew exactly why those friends had called, knew she was going to have a lot of explaining to do over the weekend.

'None of the brides actually decided to call the wedding off, did they?' Sonia prompted drily.

That had happened, more than once, with the result that they almost invariably had to start all over again a few weeks later once the bride had got over her attack of nerves and decided she wasn't marrying a monster after all!

'No, they were a pretty hardy bunch,' she answered distractedly, glancing at her watch; it was three minutes to four. She just had time to try calling Emily once again. She *had* hoped the sleepy flatmate of this morning actually might have passed on the message to

Emily that she had called, but if she had Emily had obviously been too tired to bother to call her back when she did finally get in. She had probably just assumed that Helen wanted to wish her a happy birthday, and decided it could easily wait until this evening. Emily wasn't known for her conventionality!

There was no reply at the flat at all now, and if Emily was asleep Helen knew she was wasting her time even trying to wake her; Emily would sleep through a bomb being dropped if she was tired enough.

She gratefully took a mug of tea from Sonia before rushing into her office, needing to tidy her appearance before Zack arrived. She knew that, as usual, Zack would look immaculate.

At exactly four o'clock the bell over the shop door jangled as it was opened—and Helen's nerve-endings jangled along with it!

She stood up restlessly to go out into the shop, could hear the deep tenor of Zack's voice as she approached the door, feeling herself tense at the prospect of seeing him again, even though she had known it would be inevitable very soon. She just hadn't expected it to be now!

She watched him, unobserved, from the doorway for several long seconds.

He looked the same as the last time she had seen him, time having been kind to him, dark hair flecked attractively with grey at his temples, eyes the colour of warmed chocolate surrounded by long dark lashes, his nose long and straight, mouth full-lipped but always kept firmly under control, thinning it slightly, detracting from the sensuality of that fuller lower lip, his jaw square and determined.

Today he was dressed casually, for him, obviously not having been to the hospital, although Helen knew the short-sleeved blue shirt would be made out of silk, and the black trousers that fitted low on his hips had a very precise crease down the centre of the long leg, black brogue shoes highly polished.

Tall and slender, his body nevertheless spoke of a leashed power, muscles rippling in his arms and back as he moved.

An excitingly attractive man.

A fact the young Saturday girls were well aware of as they fluttered around him, totally impervious to the fact that, at thirty-nine, Zack was old enough to be father to both of them!

But even Sonia, a much more cynical individual where men were concerned, was eyeing him with totally feminine curiosity, Helen noticed.

'My name is Neilson,' he was informing Sonia now, his voice deep and husky, and not cold as it had been when he spoke to Helen earlier. 'I'm here to see——'

'Mr Neilson,' Helen greeted smoothly, moving forward with easy grace, meeting Zack's mocking gaze with a challenge of her own as he turned to look at her with raised brows.

'Neilson?' Sonia repeated softly to herself, looking up at him with dawning comprehension. 'Then you must be——'

'The owner,' Helen cut in abruptly. 'Zack, would you like to come through to the office?' She held the door open pointedly.

He gave an acknowledging inclination of his head, dark eyes openly mocking now as he realised he had her at a disadvantage.

Helen preceded him into the adjoining room as he gave her no chance to do otherwise, standing back deliberately until she had gone through.

She could feel his gaze on her the whole time, and hoped she hadn't suddenly developed a ladder in her tights since this morning when she set out so neatly. The distance between the shop floor and her little office suddenly seemed like a mile!

'The owner, yes,' Zack echoed softly from behind her as he closed the door with a decisive click. 'But also your husband—*Mrs Neilson!*'

COLOUR flared in Helen's cheeks. 'That,' she bit out tautly, 'is only a formality, and you know it!'

'Formality or not——' Zack shrugged unconcernedly ' —the fact remains, we are husband and wife.'

'Only just,' Helen snapped. 'Another couple of months and I can apply for a divorce on the grounds of two years' separation.'

Zack's mouth twisted derisively. 'And you're counting the days!'

And the hours and minutes! God, she didn't know why she should be made to feel so defensive about wanting their divorce; the marriage itself had been a mistake from the first, a convenience, and not even of their own choosing.

Which was why she would rather it had been any other young man than Greg Neilson who had been named in this birthday joke on

Emily! Although the people responsible for the announcement couldn't have realised just what a hornets' nest they were poking; they had only lived together as a family for a matter of months, so most of Greg and Emily's friends wouldn't even realise they *were* stepbrother and stepsister.

She had known Emily and Greg still saw quite a lot of each other socially—of course she had; it had been inevitable when they were both attending the same college, and obviously the friendship had given their friends a good idea for a practical joke.

With *any* other boy but Greg even Helen might have found it funny!

She moved to sit behind the small desk, which was all she could get inside this room, feeling more self-assured as she took on her business mantle. 'I'm sure you aren't here today to discuss our divorce——'

'Are you?' His voice was silkily soft, as he moved with the minimum of effort needed to take him to the chair placed opposite hers, his height looking slightly ridiculous folded into the small wooden chair.

She sighed. 'Zack——'

'Emily and Greg,' he intercepted drily. 'What are we going to do about them?'

'Do about them?' she echoed in a puzzled voice. 'We aren't going to *do* anything about them.' She shook her head derisively. 'Their friends are all having a good laugh at their expense because of Emily's birthday to-day——'

'I'm well aware of the fact that it's my stepdaughter's eighteenth birthday today,' he bit out harshly.

'Emily is *not* your stepdaughter!' Two bright spots of angry colour heightened her cheeks.

His mouth tightened. 'Oh, yes, she is, Helen. And she always will be. Whether you like it or not,' he challenged hardly. 'Whether you go through with the divorce or not——'

'Of course I'll go through with the divorce!' There was no doubt about that.

'Why?' Zack watched her with narrowed, questioning eyes, no longer the colour of warmed chocolate, so dark now, they were almost black.

Her eyes widened. 'Why?' she echoed. 'But——' She shook her head dismissively. 'We're straying from the point of your visit.'

'Are we?' He crossed one long leg over the other, perfectly relaxed, filled with that stillness that was so unnerving.

'Zack, I've had a busy day.' And her head was starting to pound! This man always had been able to tie her up in knots.

'Of course,' he acknowledged coldly. 'Heaven forbid I should interrupt your working day about something as trivial as our children's engagement!'

He was trying to make her feel guilty again! 'I've already told you that it's all nonsense,' she snapped. 'Just a not very funny joke.'

'You seem so convinced of that, but I don't see how you can be so sure.' He shook his head. 'Or have you spoken to Emily?' His eyes were narrowed.

'Well, no, but——' She frowned. 'I've called her at home a couple of times,' she added defensively. 'She hasn't been at home.'

Zack nodded slowly. 'Greg has been equally elusive . . .'

'When I see her tonight we can all have a good laugh about it,' Helen dismissed, although she didn't think her father would find it in the least amusing; he had never approved of Zack, and Greg was Zack's son . . .

'So we can,' Zack drawled. 'Won't it be a jolly way to start the evening?' he taunted.

Helen became suddenly still, staring at him as a terrible possibility occurred to her. 'Emily invited you and Greg to join us for dinner tonight...?' But she already knew the answer, could see it in Zack's face.

'Yes, she—and she didn't tell you she had done so, the little minx,' he slowly realised at Helen's distraught expression.

Deliberately so, Helen knew; Emily had known that although she had always got on with Greg she certainly wouldn't want Zack there. She knew exactly what her daughter had done, that she had invited Zack and Greg and then telephoned her favourite Chinese restaurant herself to change the booking from three to five people, without telling Helen she had done it.

The problem was that Emily had adored Zack from the first. Never having known her real father because he had died while she was still only a baby, it had been easy for the fifteen-year-old Emily had been when Helen and Zack had married to accept him as a father figure.

Helen knew, belatedly, that it should have occurred to her before that Emily might want Zack at her birthday party—her *family* birthday party.

Zack watched the emotions flickering across the paleness of her face with narrowed eyes. 'Helen, I meet Emily for lunch at least every couple of weeks,' he told her softly. 'And she visits the house often, goes up to her bedroom, lies on the bed, listens to music——'

'Her bedroom is at my house!' Helen burst out tautly, shaken by what he was telling her, each word like the prick of a knife against her skin. 'And you knew damn well I wouldn't want you at this dinner tonight; you could have——'

'*You* wouldn't want?' he echoed, dangerously soft, giving her a pitying glance. 'I don't think Emily's eighteenth birthday celebrations should have anything to do with what *you* want! When we got married we didn't just marry each other; the children were involved too,' he reminded her coldly. 'And my relationship with Emily has survived the separation; I intend for it to remain that way,' he informed her in a voice that brooked no argument.

Helen sensed his criticism of her own relationship with Greg. She had been very fond of her stepson, had deeply regretted not being able to maintain their friendship, at least. But at the time she had thought, whether rightly or wrongly, that a clean break was the best way.

She had had no idea that Emily had kept up such a close relationship with Zack, had always believed that she and Emily had a close mother-daughter relationship, that Emily could tell her anything. My God, she thought, no wonder Zack had been so scornful of that claim earlier today; *he* had known the truth.

It hurt, badly, that she had been so wrong about that. It hurt even more to acknowledge that she had created that particular situation herself, with her own reluctance to even have Zack's name mentioned in her presence. As Zack so rightly said, their children had been involved in their marriage too, and they had feelings that couldn't be turned on and off on command.

'Oh, God,' Helen groaned, burying her face in her hands. 'What a mess!'

She had married Zack, she had truly believed at the time, for all the right reasons, and look what it had done to her beloved daughter. Not that Emily had actually been reduced to lying to her about the lunches and the visits to Zack's house; she had just omitted ever to mention them. And that had probably only been done so as not to hurt Helen.

'Helen, I—— For God's sake!' Zack swore as she flinched away from the touch of his hand on her shoulder. 'You don't have to make your aversion to me quite so obvious, damn it,' he rasped. 'I was only trying to comfort you!'

She hadn't even been aware of his approach until she felt the warmth of his hand through the material of her blouse, and then she had reacted as if she had received an electric shock.

Now Zack was looking at her with that mixture of disgust and frustration that had been such a part of their marriage, his hands thrust out of harm's way into the pockets of his trousers, stretching the material tautly across his thighs.

'I'm sorry,' Helen said abruptly as she looked quickly away. 'I—it's been a difficult day for me.'

He continued to look at her for several long, tension-filled minutes, and then he relaxed slightly, his mouth twisting derisively. 'Not the least of it being my coming here.'

She began to breathe normally again as he moved away. 'Not the least,' she acknowledged tautly. 'And as it seems we shall be seeing you this evening——'

'Greg, too,' he put in softly, raising innocent brows as she gave him a quelling look.

'Greg, too,' she repeated in a carefully controlled voice, hoping Emily hadn't decided to invite other 'guests' she didn't know about; she was going to have to sit down and have a serious talk with her daughter, and about so much more than the repercussions of that ridiculous announcement in the newspaper this morning—although God knew that was serious enough! 'As you will both be joining us for dinner this evening, that seems as good a time as any to discuss the engagement announcement,' she dismissed, wanting to put an end to this conversation; usually so calm and in control, she always changed when Zack was around.

'And how quickly you can get a retraction printed,' Zack drily guessed what she hadn't yet had a chance to say.

Grey eyes met his coolly. 'But of course.'

'Of course,' he echoed tautly, moving to the door. 'We'll see you later, then,' he taunted, pausing with his hand on the door-handle. 'Oh, and, Helen—just be grateful that no one added to the confusion by announcing the daughter of Mrs H. *Neilson* was to marry the son of Mr Z. Neilson!' And with that last mocking parting shot he left, the bell over the shop door ringing seconds later to show that he hadn't lingered outside.

Mrs Neilson; she had hardly been that long enough for the ink to dry on their marriage certificate! She had certainly had no difficulty reverting back to the name of Palmer after their separation.

There was the briefest of knocks before Sonia put her head round the side of the door. 'Everything OK?' she frowned.

Evidence of just how brief her marriage to Zack had been was that this woman, with whom Helen had worked for almost two years, had no idea of its existence! She and Zack had already been separated when she took Sonia on as her assistant, and there had been no reason since that time to mention that she had once been married—was still *technically* married—to their landlord.

But at least that last fact gave her an excuse to explain Zack's presence here at all. 'Just checking up on his investment,' Helen dismissed with a shrug.

Unfortunately that seemed to alarm Sonia rather than reassure her, probably because Zack hadn't deemed it necessary to pay them a visit in the previous two years!

'Problems?' She came into the office and closed the door behind her, inviting confidences if Helen wanted to give them. 'There's nothing wrong with the lease, is there?'

Ironically it was this shop that had first caused her to be involved with Zack's family at all. 'No,' she answered ruefully. 'I think we may as well close up for the day, don't you?' she suggested brightly.

As this was the first time she had ever known Helen to suggest closing up early, Sonia looked even more concerned.

'If anyone asks why——' Helen's mouth twisted wryly '—tell them it's my daughter's eighteenth birthday!'

Sonia's frown instantly cleared. 'Oh, God, yes, I'd forgotten. You'll want time to get ready to go out tonight,' she realised, hurrying off to begin the closing-up process for over the rest of the weekend.

Helen's smile faded, her depression returning with a vengeance once she was alone again. She had been looking forward to this evening for a long time, to quietly celebrating her daughter's coming-of-age, and now it had taken on an air of oppression which she found totally demoralising.

Another thing she found totally depressing was the thought of wearing her reliable black gown to go out in. It was over five years old, and while it had classical lines and was obviously of good quality she had worn it on several occasions in Zack's company in the past. And the last thing she wanted was to start the evening feeling at a disadvantage. Damn him!

It was only four-thirty now—good God, it had seemed a lot longer than twenty-five minutes when Zack was actually here!—so there was another hour before most of the dress shops in the area would close.

Stubbornness, at feeling forced into the position of needing to look her best tonight, and pride, because as she had no real choice about being in Zack's company she had to look her very best, for her own sake, both warred within her.

But not for long! Stubbornness had never got her very far where Zack was concerned, and her pride was one of the few things she had left.

'I'll be back in time to lock up,' she assured Sonia as she rushed through the shop on the way out to her car.

She was slightly above average height, slender, a standard size ten, so should have had no trouble finding something for a quiet family celebration.

And yet nothing she tried on in the first two shops looked right. As usual, she was convinced that when she saw the right dress she would know it was the one. Unfortunately, she never did, which was why she had held on to her reliable black for so long! And tonight, when she didn't have time to dither, was no exception; nothing transformed her into the regally confident beauty she would have liked to be.

It was ridiculous anyway, she scolded herself impatiently as she pulled a thin blue woollen dress over her head and smoothed its softness down over her hips. Who was she hoping to impress? Certainly not Zack; he had made *his* opinion of her more than obvious over the years. And she was tired, and hot, and totally fed up with the whole stupid——

She knew without question that this dress was *the* one!

She had looked up uninterestedly to her reflection in the mirror on the changing-room wall, and was stunned by the transformation that the just-above-knee-length dress made. Oh, she didn't look regal, nor especially confident or beautiful; what she did look was— sexy!

On the hanger the thin cashmere dress had looked unimpressive, but Helen had been attracted to the royal blue colour, if nothing else, and the sales assistant, seeing at least a spark of interest, had encouraged her to try it on.

The short style showed off a long expanse of her slender, shapely legs, the soft wool moulding gently, if not exactly clinging, to the curves of her body. The sleeves reached down to her wrists, the neck softly encircled her throat, and yet there was an underlying sensuality about the way the dress moved with her, and it made her hair appear almost black, her eyes no longer grey but seeming to take on a reflective blue.

'I'll take it,' she decided before she had a chance to talk herself out of it.

The sales assistant looked relieved, and Helen couldn't exactly blame her; it was almost five-thirty on a Saturday night, after all.

She had bought the dress, even been persuaded into buying a pair of sheer Lycra tights to wear with it, and was driving back to lock up her own shop when reaction set in; she had never, ever bought anything that actually made her look *sexy*. Businesslike, smart, hopefully attractive, but never *sexy*.

Her shoulders slumped as she realised that it would have to be the reliable black after all; her father and Emily would wonder what on earth had come over her if she went out in the clinging blue dress. And God knew what Zack would make of it!

She ran a weary hand over her eyes; thank God that particular brainstorm had passed!

'My God, Helen, I hardly recognised you; you look beautiful!'

She spun around self-consciously, the high colour that had been due to anger seconds ago, when she'd entered the restaurant, now changing to something quite different as she saw the look in Zack's eyes when he openly stared at her.

She was wearing the royal blue cashmere dress!

She hadn't intended to, had taken her old reliable black one from the wardrobe after showering and washing her hair, and taken it down to the kitchen to press when her father came into the room, already dressed and ready to go out in his best dark blue suit, iron-grey hair brushed severely back from his face.

Helen's conscience had pricked her into telling him that Zack and Greg would be at the dinner tonight. The last thing she needed was her father collapsing at the restaurant when the other two men arrived, and it was a possibility if he hadn't been warned.

His reaction to the news was to refuse to go to the dinner himself—'if that man was going to be there'!

She should have expected it, of course. But even so, she had thought, for Emily's sake if nothing else, that her father would make the effort and go.

But no amount of cajoling on Helen's part could persuade him to change his mind. Reasoning either. Or sheer frustrated anger. Her father was adamant: if Zack was going to be there tonight, then he wasn't.

Helen didn't know which one to be angrier with, Zack for accepting the invitation and so creating the situation in the first place—he could have avoided going tonight without hurting Emily's feelings too much, if he had tried, and he had to know the dissension it would cause among the family!—or her father for adding to the problem by behaving so stubbornly.

In the end it didn't really matter which of them was to blame; she felt totally agitated, throwing aside the black dress when she realised how late it had become while she tried to persuade her father, defiantly putting on the blue cashmere. It was bad enough that she

was going to have to make excuses for her
father's absence that would satisfy Emily, but
for her to be late on top of that would be unforgivable.

Sheer frustration with the whole situation
had been enough to instil a certain amount of
bravado into her actions; her hair was brushed
back in a casually wind-swept style, her make-
up was slightly heavier than usual, her lashes
long and thick from the mascara she had liberally applied, her lids shaded with blue
shadow, her lip-gloss a deeper red than she
wore in the day, making her lips fuller.

As she faced Zack across the reception area
of the restaurant she knew she looked grace-
fully tall and slender, the heels on her black
shoes adding to her height, her dark colouring against the blue of the dress a startling
contrast. It was obvious from the speculation
in Zack's gaze as he slowly looked her up and
down that he was very aware of the change in
her appearance.

He looked as assuredly attractive as he
usually did, in a dark suit and snowy white
shirt, the latter making his skin look darkly
tanned; he was standing across from her with
an ease that was totally deceptive, Helen

knew, leashed power in the wide shoulders and tapered thighs, exuding an air of masculinity that was completely unaffected.

Helen wondered how she had ever allowed herself to enter into the sort of marriage she had with this man. She must have been mad!

'Not that you don't always look beautiful.' His mouth twisted wryly as he realised what he had said to her in greeting.

'Stop back-pedalling, Zack,' she derided. 'We both know how I usually look.' And it was nothing like this!

As he moved to her side, the light overhead caught in the darkness of his hair, giving it an ebony sheen, dark hair that was still damp from having been recently washed. Helen knew that Zack would have showered before coming out tonight, had his second shave of the day. The fact that she knew his movements so intimately unsettled her even further.

'Why do you always have to put yourself down in that way?' he rasped now, standing so close that she could smell his aftershave, that elusively masculine smell that was so much a part of him. She could never recognise the smell of this aftershave on other men without thinking of Zack; it could be very disconcerting. 'I've never denied you're a beautiful woman,' he told her abruptly.

Helen had never been very impressed with the way she looked, had never actually had a lot of time, with a job to do and a small child to bring up, to take a lot of notice of it. And the truth of it was, the way she looked had made no difference in either of her marriages; they had both been disasters. Her first marriage had been entered into when she was too young to know what she was doing, and the second marriage—that was too complicated to even think about!

'And you know about beautiful women, don't you, Zack?' she derided drily.

His eyes narrowed coldly. 'And just what is that supposed to mean?' His voice was soft, dangerously so.

Braver people than her had been quelled beneath the power of that withering gaze, and in fact it took all of her will-power not to be counted among their number, but she couldn't allow herself to be cowed by this man. 'You know very well——'

'We're a mere two minutes late and already they're at each other's throats,' remarked a lightly mocking voice.

She and Zack had been so engrossed in their conversation that neither of them had been aware of Greg and Emily entering the restaurant together, looking at the two of *them* with the indulgent affection usually shown towards recalcitrant children!

Zack met his son's gaze challengingly, and if Helen had been going to make a reply it was never uttered as she watched in mute fascination while Emily turned laughingly to Greg, her hand resting briefly against his arm as she did so. Her left hand. And on the third finger of that hand winked a diamond and emerald ring.

An engagement ring...?

CHAPTER THREE

'MUMMY, you look marvellous!' Emily
moved forward to hug her, long dark hair
cascading wildly almost to her waist, briefly
enveloping Helen in its perfumed silkiness.
She moved back, green eyes admiring as she
looked at Helen, still clasping her hands
lightly in hers. 'New dress?'

Helen had always marvelled at how she had
managed to produce this gloriously beautiful
creature, Emily being petite in the extreme,
fresh and beautiful in a typically English rose
type of way: clear creamy complexion that
needed no make-up, green eyes glowing with
health and vitality, her only artificial colouring the dark red lip-gloss. And somehow
Emily could wear anything and still look
wonderful—even the loose black lace dress
she wore tonight, which didn't quite reach her
ankles, and the flat black ballet-type slip-
pers. On anyone else the outfit would have

looked drab and shapeless; Emily just looked vivaciously lovely.

Helen was so proud of her ethereally beautiful daughter, had always found it difficult to be stern with her only offspring, but with that ring sparkling on Emily's finger she couldn't afford to be indulgent. 'Yes, it's a new dress, Emily, as I'm sure you're very aware.' She mocked her daughter's delaying tactic. 'But I don't think——'

'You look gorgeous, Helen.' Greg kissed her warmly on the cheek. 'Doesn't she, Dad?' He looked challengingly at his father.

Zack's mouth twisted wryly. 'We've already discussed Helen's appearance before the two of you arrived,' he dismissed. 'Now I suggest we go and sit at our table; we're blocking up the entrance,' he added pointedly as a group of people came in the door and tried to get past them.

'Zack.' Emily's face lit up with pleasure as she kissed him warmly on the cheek. 'You look as handsome as ever,' she teased.

'Shift, young lady!' He tapped her lightly on the bottom as the waiter came to show them to their table. 'The charm isn't going to work tonight,' he warned darkly, shooting his son a cautioning look too, nodding for the younger couple to precede them into the dining area, and taking a firm grip of Helen's arm so that they walked in side by side.

A united front. How was that for a first? Although that wasn't altogether fair to Zack; he had always listened to her point of view, even if he rarely agreed with it! And she wasn't completely sure how he felt about this latest development, although she knew he couldn't have missed that ring sparkling on Emily's finger.

She had to admit, when she looked at Emily and Greg as they walked ahead of them, they made an attractive couple, Emily so delicately beautiful, Greg looking like a blond god at her side. Greg had inherited his colouring from his mother, long hair gleaming golden on to his shoulders; he moved with the grace of a natural athlete, the baggy suit he wore not detracting from his animal grace.

Emily and Greg looked so right together. Strange, Helen had never noticed that before...

Zack's hand tightened on her arm, his fingers hurting her through the thin wool. 'God, you're so transparent!' he rasped disgustedly.

She looked up at him, still dazed by the direction her thoughts had taken.

'I doubt you would be so disapproving if Greg weren't my son!' he scorned, releasing her so abruptly that she momentarily lost her balance.

The accusation was so far removed from what she had actually been thinking that it took her several seconds to turn her attention to what he had said.

And in part he was wrong; she would have disapproved of Emily being engaged to anyone now, believed her daughter was far too young to be seriously involved with anyone just yet. The fact that the young man involved *was* Greg did make the situation more difficult. And as yet neither of them had offered any explanation for that ring on Emily's left hand.

Helen kept trying not to look at it as Emily sat down, but as if to mock and taunt her the candle in the centre of the table seemed to make every facet gleam brighter than ever!

Helen's eyes flashed as she turned to Zack before sitting down. 'But he *is* your son,' she bit out so softly that only he could hear.

He returned her gaze coldly. 'And how you hate the very thought of it,' he muttered his distaste for her prejudice before sitting in the chair next to hers.

Of course she hated the thought of it; he couldn't seriously expect her to be thrilled at the prospect of possibly being forced to accept his continued presence in their lives—as Emily's father-in-law this time! Good God, there was another possibility she hadn't even thought of; if—and it was still a big if as far as she was concerned, despite the existence of that ring on Emily's finger!—Emily and Greg really were engaged, and eventually married and had children, she and Zack would be their respective grandparents!

She had believed, *hoped*, that once her divorce from Zack became final she could forget the marriage had ever taken place at all. This unforeseen situation could make that impossible!

The sooner she established exactly what was going on between Emily and Greg, the better!

'Helen believes,' Zack drawled before she could speak, his gaze raking over her derisively before he turned his attention to the young couple, 'that the announcement in *The Times* this morning was a practical joke.'

Greg's hand moved to clasp Emily's in a protective gesture as it rested on top of the white cotton tablecloth. 'And you?' he challenged almost defiantly.

'I think——' Zack looked perfectly relaxed as he leaned back in his chair, but that very stillness could hide a dozen emotions, all of them ominous, as Helen very well knew '—that you owe us some sort of explanation. Don't you?' He arched one dark brow.

'Not *now*, Zack,' Emily protested.

'Now,' he insisted firmly.

'But it's my birthday,' she pouted prettily. 'And I—Mummy, where's Gramps?' she frowned suddenly. 'I thought when we arrived that he must be in the loo, but—he isn't here, is he?' she realised flatly.

Helen knew that Zack was looking at her, could feel the hard query of his gaze, and she determinedly did not look at him. He knew of the dislike her father had for him, of how stubborn the older man could be, although she had never been able to fault Zack's behaviour towards her father; he had always treated him with respect, no matter what the provocation might have been to do otherwise!

Emily was still looking at her frowningly. 'Don't tell me,' she sighed. 'He wasn't feeling well!'

'Emily!' She reproved the sarcastic edge to her daughter's voice. 'You know your grandfather doesn't enjoy good health.'

'On the contrary,' Zack put in softly, 'he enjoys *ill*-health.'

'You have no right——' Helen broke off abruptly as the waiter came to take their order, the delay while they ordered giving her time to get herself back under control. Emily's disappointment was understandable, but Zack's derision was unforgivable.

'Gramps didn't come,' Emily repeated dully, once the waiter had departed, turning away to talk softly to Greg, but not before Helen had seen the sheen of tears in her eyes.

Helen knew her father was in the wrong for behaving so stubbornly and ruining Emily's birthday, but she also found Zack's attitude extremely annoying. She was so agitated that as she took out her napkin to place it over her knee it dropped to the floor.

Zack bent down to retrieve it for her, his gaze clearly mocking her slightly flustered movements. 'Your father heard of the return of the prodigal, did he, and decided not to come?' he taunted softly.

'You're hardly that!' she snapped disparagingly.

He held her gaze in steady challenge as he placed the napkin in her lap, his fingers deliberately brushing against her thigh, and laughed softly as Helen pushed his hand away with a hurried movement, high colour in her cheeks.

Helen was breathing shallowly, inwardly berating herself for letting this man's touch affect her in that way. She suddenly wished that the champagne Zack had ordered would arrive; she desperately needed something to steady her nerves!

Zack turned to the young couple. 'We seem to have strayed off the subject of your supposed engagement,' he reminded them firmly.

Emily instantly brightened. 'Oh, there's nothing "supposed" about it.' She held out her left hand so that they could all see the ring sparkling there. 'Greg and I went out and bought this today.' She moved her hand so that the emerald and surrounding diamonds winked more effectively.

Which was why neither of them had been at home all day to answer the telephone! Or was it? Helen had rung too early the first time this morning for the shops to even be open. She had the distinct feeling that she and Zack had been given the run-around all day by their respective children, Emily and Greg putting off the moment of confrontation until it couldn't be put off any longer.

'You put the announcement in the newspaper yourselves,' Helen guessed impatiently. 'Emily, how could you?'

'Mummy, there was no other way.' Emily looked at her imploringly. 'If we had come to you first and told you——'

'*Asking* might have been better,' Zack put in harshly. 'It's customary to at least ask the girl's parents first before making any other plans,' he reproved his son sternly.

'You two certainly didn't ask Gramps,' Emily accused. 'Otherwise the two of you would never have got married!'

'Emily!' Helen gasped weakly, mortified at even having that particular relationship between Zack and herself brought into the conversation.

'Well, it's the truth,' her daughter asserted defensively. 'And *if* we had come to the two of you and told you how we felt about each other you would only have put every objection you could think of in our way.'

'Only because you're too young to know your own minds,' Helen defended exasperatedly. 'Both of you!' Greg might be possessed of his father's supreme self-confidence, but he was still, after all, only nineteen.

'You were both married at our ages,' Greg pointed out reasoningly.

Not to each other, thank God, Helen sighed with inward relief.

'And it was far from a perfect arrangement,' Zack told them impatiently. 'Helen believes she married too young, I know. And your mother and I struggled along as students, Greg, because my parents had disapproved of the marriage at the time. It became even more of a struggle after you were born.' He shook his head at the memory of the hardship involved in being a medical student and trying to be a father at the same time.

'Thanks!' Greg drawled hardly, blue eyes glittering as angrily as his father's.

'You know damn well I didn't mean it that way,' Zack snapped.

'I know that what you're saying sounds suspiciously like a threat to me,' Greg glared. 'Stay away from each other or we'll leave you to struggle like we had to, is what you mean!'

Helen looked at the two men with dismay; they were too much alike, these two, and as she had often had to do in the past she found herself cutting in between them in an effort to ward off a serious disagreement. 'Your father wasn't suggesting that at all, Greg,' she soothed. 'He——'

'Wasn't I?' Brown eyes glittered coldly. 'They *are* too damned young to know what they're doing!'

'And I suppose you're always so confident you're doing the right thing?' Greg challenged defiantly. 'That's why the two of you only stayed married to each other for five months!'

'Greg!' Emily gasped warningly, turning concernedly to Helen as she paled, very wisely not even daring to look at Zack, although the anger emanating from him was a tangible thing, to all of them. 'Mummy, I'm sorry Greg said that; he didn't mean it.' She glared across the table at him as he would have disagreed with her, his mouth setting mutinously as he bit back his angry retort. 'But just because your teenage marriages turned out to be less than ideal, it doesn't mean that ours will,' she added with persuasive charm. 'Greg and I love each other.'

'Love, at that age, isn't always enough,' Zack rasped, some of his anger turning to amusement as Greg bit back his burning retort to that challenge when Emily looked at him warningly once again. 'Although sometimes it can be,' he drawled at his son's obvious subservience to his new fiancée.

Helen frowned as she sensed Greg's anger was about to erupt over once again, and turned to Emily. 'How soon were you thinking of marrying...?' From the way her daughter was talking, it didn't sound as if the young couple planned a long engagement; Greg would cease being a 'teenager' in November!

'We thought September.' Emily gave the glowering Greg a glowing smile.

'But that's only three months away!' Helen gasped disbelievingly. 'Emily, you—you aren't pregnant, are you?' Oh, please God, no, not her daughter too!

'Of course not.' Emily was indignant at the very idea. 'Being pregnant is no reason to get married—anyway, it certainly isn't the reason Greg and I want to get married in September.'

Helen accepted the rebuke for what it was, but she could have told Emily that things were done very differently eighteen years ago, that family pressure on a very young girl could indeed make marriage more than a possibility when that young girl had made the mistake of getting herself pregnant on her very first fumbling encounter with a boy. Especially when that 'family pressure' came in the form of her own grandfather...

'Emily, you were going to university in September,' she reminded her daughter abruptly, pushing those memories to the back of her mind. As she had for the last eighteen years. Perhaps if Ian hadn't died when Emily was only six months old, if there had been wedding anniversaries to explain away... But there hadn't, and so Emily had never learnt that she had been born a mere six months after her parents married. As the years had passed there had seemed no reason to tell her. As far as Helen was concerned, there still wasn't.

But as she looked up and saw Zack watching her with those all-seeing brown eyes she knew that it was a possibility that had occurred to him!

'I still am,' Emily answered brightly, drawing Helen's attention—thankfully!—away from Zack. 'Getting married isn't going to change any of that. We can have it all nowadays, Mummy—the career and marriage.' She gave Greg a dreamy smile.

It had always been possible to 'have it all', but it was never without sacrificing other things that also mattered! But she could see from Emily's rapt expression that she wouldn't listen to any of that at this moment in time.

And September was the time Helen had intended applying for her divorce from Zack. It was ridiculous; their children would be marrying during the same month their parents were divorced! She couldn't help wondering if that idea had even occurred to Zack. But she knew that, like her, he wanted the divorce.

'Emily——' She broke off as the champagne arrived, quickly followed by their food, and champagne was poured out all round as they toasted Emily's birthday. Helen emptied her glass completely; at that moment she needed it!

Her glass was instantly refilled, and she raised that to her lips to take another sip, her gaze clashing with Zack's as she did so, his smile mocking before he turned to order another bottle of champagne. Well, what did he expect? she fumed inwardly. All of this was enough to turn anyone to drink!

Zack waited until the waiter had finally departed, after laying out the selection of food in the centre of the table, before speaking on a personal level again. 'September is out,' he told Greg hardly.

He had remembered! Helen didn't think she could have heard the last from him on the subject, especially after Greg's mutinous outburst concerning the two of them.

Greg eyed him suspiciously. 'Why?'

His father shrugged. 'I'm going to be away for the whole of September. In the States. On a lecture tour.'

And so he wouldn't even be in England to receive the divorce papers, Helen realised with some dismay. So much for thinking he might find it a little odd too to be going through a divorce in the midst of their children's wedding plans. She should have known better!

But she supposed his absence at that time did mean that they should be able to persuade Emily and Greg to delay any wedding plans for a month or two...

As Zack watched her with mocking eyes she knew he had been very much aware of the fact that their divorce should go through in September, and her thoughts on it just now. It was obvious that her frustration at having things delayed in this way caused him not one jot of remorse, that he found her disappointment amusing.

'Lucky you.' She deliberately kept her voice light. 'Anywhere nice?'

'Florida,' he supplied drily, not fooled for a moment by her attempted unconcern.

'All that sunshine!' And no doubt he would find ample time to deepen his tan. It was disturbing to remember that two years ago that tan had been all-over...

'Why not come with me, Helen?' he invited softly. 'We could have a second honeymoon.'

Considering there had never been a first one, that might be a little difficult!

'We are still married, after all,' he added provocatively, taunting her with the knowledge that by that time they really shouldn't have been.

'Oh, what a lovely idea!' Emily was the one to answer excitedly before Helen could make any reply. 'Do go, Mummy,' she encouraged. 'You would have a lovely time.'

With Zack? Helen didn't think so. Just as she knew she wasn't supposed to take the suggestion seriously, it was just Zack's warped sense of humour in action! 'Don't be silly, Emily,' she dismissed briskly. 'Zack was only teasing.'

He raised dark brows, and for one breathless moment Helen thought he was going to deny her statement.

He held her gaze for long timeless seconds, his eyes dark, and then the moment passed as he leant forward to replenish her glass himself this time.

Helen swallowed hard, picking up the glass to throw the champagne to the back of her throat in a gesture of defiance, vaguely realising that she shouldn't have done, that she hadn't eaten anything since her slice of toast at breakfast this morning, that she was starting to feel slightly light-headed.

It was unusual for her to drink at all, but she knew that if she wanted to get through this evening at all this was the only way she was going to do it. Unusual circumstances called for drastic measures, and even the most insensitive person would have to admit that this dinner party was unusual: her estranged husband, and the newly engaged couple, her daughter and his son. It was enough to turn a saint to drink!

As the meal progressed, and her glass was refilled almost as soon as she had taken a sip from it, she had to admit that the light-headedness began to increase, so that in the end she began to feel very strange indeed. For one thing the conversation at the table seemed to be passing over her head as she had trouble focusing on the other three people seated here, let alone concentrating on what they were actually saying.

And Zack had taken on a curiously sensual aura; just looking at him sent a thrill of pleasure through her body. He really was the most attractive man, emitting a sensuality that only hinted at the pleasure promised in his arms, and——

Oh, God, she was drunk!

She had thrown all caution to the wind and inwardly admitted her attraction towards Zack, so she must be drunk. She began to giggle as she realised the method by which she had come to that momentous conclusion, putting a hand up self-consciously to cover her mouth as Emily, Greg and Zack all turned to look at her enquiringly; they hadn't been discussing anything remotely funny, that much was obvious!

'I'm sorry.' She did her best to look seriously attentive, but as she had no idea what they had been talking about she found that more than a little difficult! 'I just—I didn't——' She gave another giggle.

'I think it's time I drove you home,' Zack said firmly, signalling for the bill to be brought over to him.

Helen kept her eyes open wide in an effort to look alert—although in reality she was starting to feel decidedly sleepy. 'But I came in my own car,' she protested.

'I know,' he drawled. 'That's why I'm going to drive you home!'

She watched as he made a cheque out for the bill, suddenly realising that she should be the one doing that, reaching down beside her chair in search of her handbag and her own cheque-book.

'Don't,' Zack warned softly, barely loud enough for her to hear at all, but his tone brooked no argument. 'Can we drop you two off anywhere?' He looked across at Emily and Greg.

Greg shook his head. 'We're meeting some friends to continue the celebrations,' he refused lightly. 'Are you going to be able to manage?' He was looking indulgently at Helen as he spoke while she concentrated—very hard!—on trying to get a tissue from her bag.

The catch on her bag, now that she had finally attained the troublesome tissue, was proving just as difficult, and the more she tried to close it, the more impossible it became. What was wrong with the thing?

'Let me.' Zack took the bag from her agitated fingers, closing the catch at the first attempt. 'I'll manage,' he told Greg drily.

As he always 'managed', Helen thought a little resentfully. He was one of the most capable men she knew, didn't seem to need anyone. He certainly didn't need a wife, not any more!

She looked up with a frown as Emily and Greg stood up. 'Oh, are you going?' she said disappointedly, wondering why her voice sounded as if it were coming through cotton wool. She shook her head dismissively; of course it wasn't!

'And so are we,' Zack informed her derisively, standing up to pull back her chair for her, putting out a hand to clasp her arm as she would have swayed. 'And don't think my conversation with the two of you is over,' he warned the young couple as he clamped Helen firmly to his side.

Greg instantly took on a defensive stance, Emily a slightly guilty one.

'Tonight just isn't the time to continue it,' Zack added grimly as Helen watched them all with slightly dazed eyes.

She was trying very hard to concentrate, but at the moment she couldn't even remember what conversation Zack was talking about. All she knew was that it seemed a very long way to the door!

But it didn't seem quite so far away with Zack's guiding arm about her waist.

It was amazing how cared-for the warmth of that arm made her feel, cosseted, protected, her body pressed into the side of Zack's, her softness against his hardness. How incredibly good that felt!

She turned to thank him as they went outside. But she didn't get the chance as the fresh air almost burst her lungs with its clarity, her legs buckling beneath her, and she clutched out at Zack as the pavement spun up towards her.

But she never made contact with that concrete, for that arm tightened about her waist and pulled her up hard against Zack's chest. And suddenly she felt dizzy again, her breath catching shallowly in her chest as she looked straight up into Zack's granite-hewn face, her eyes on a level with the firmness of his jaw. And the full sensuality of his lips. Those lips slightly parted. So near. So very near...

''Night, you two,' he spoke past her, making her aware of the fact that Greg and Emily had followed them out of the restaurant. 'I'll ring you in the morning, Greg,' he added firmly. 'Make sure you're in this time.' The last was added warningly, just in case Greg should try avoiding him as he and Helen were sure he had today, Emily too.

Helen looked at the young couple slowly, still slightly dazed by how tempted she had been seconds ago to raise her lips to Zack's, to feel the firmness of those lips against hers. Emily was looking at her with approval for her close proximity to Zack, if she knew her daughter at all!

'Lovely evening, Mummy.' Emily moved to kiss her on the cheek. 'See you tomorrow,' she added before strolling off with Greg at her side.

Tomorrow? What was happening tomorrow?

Zack looked down at her indulgently as he saw the complete lack of comprehension on her face. 'Don't worry about it, Helen,' he advised softly, his arm still supportively about her waist. 'I'll explain it all to you later.'

His car was parked next to hers in the restaurant car park, a sleek Jaguar, a newer model than the one she remembered him driving in the past, but the interior was just as luxurious, and Helen sank down into her seat with a contented sigh, loving the smell of new leather.

' "Home, James" ,' she instructed silkily, snuggling down into the leather, the engine nothing more than a gentle purr—to match her own!

Zack laughed softly in the darkness. 'I think maybe I should have plied you with champagne years ago!'

'Hm?' Her lids felt too heavy for her even to lift them.

'Never mind,' he murmured, and then gently orchestrated music filled the air, so beautifully soothing, so relaxing.

Helen woke with a start, realising that she must have drifted off to sleep almost as soon as they began the drive home, because it seemed like only seconds later that the engine being switched off alerted her subconscious to the fact that they had stopped.

'Home, madam,' Zack told her gruffly, turning to look at her, his arm along the back of her seat.

'That was a perfectly painless evening, wasn't it?' she said with some relief, searching for the door-handle—and not having much luck! Where was the thing? She frowned.

'More so for some than others,' he mocked softly before getting out of the car and coming round to her side to open her door for her. 'Careful,' he warned as she stepped unsteadily out on to the pavement.

She smiled dreamily as she looked up at the stars. 'Isn't it a beautifully clear night?'

'Beautifully,' he echoed drily. 'Has champagne always had this effect on you?' he asked with deceptive mildness on the walk up to the house.

She frowned with the effort of trying to remember the last time she had had champagne; their wedding certainly hadn't been a cause for celebration, so she knew that they hadn't had it then!

'I'm really not sure,' she said slowly. 'Anyway,' she dismissed, glowing up at him, 'I feel wonderful tonight! Thank you so much for driving me home, Zack.' She turned fully to face him as they reached the door. 'It was very kind of you.'

'Not at all,' he returned smoothly, lightly mocking her attempt at formality.

Helen looked up at him in the moonlight, wondering what he was waiting for, if he intended kissing her goodnight. And then she chided herself for even thinking he might want to; they were getting a divorce, and people who were getting divorced didn't *kiss* each other!

She gave him another over-bright smile. 'Don't let me keep you.'

He still made no effort to move. 'You aren't.'

'It must be late.' She moistened her lips. 'I'm sure you must want to get home.'

He took his hand out of his pocket, raising it towards Helen, and for a moment she wasn't sure what he intended doing. But that hand continued on past her, and Helen heard the key he held enter the lock, turning, then the door pushed gently open behind her.

She looked at him dazedly. 'How did you——?' She turned in amazement to look at the open door, gasping as full realisation finally dawned on her.

'I *am* home, Helen.' He was so close now that his breath warmed her cheek.

And she could see that he was, that it was his house he had driven them both back to and not the one she shared with her father. The question was, why?

'Ah, Helen.' He spoke softly, brown eyes warm as his gaze rested on her slightly parted lips. 'You really do look beautiful tonight.'

'I do?' She looked up at him with limpid eyes. 'I mean—I *do*?' She tried to sound less breathless as she realised she was flirting, with her own husband. With *Zack*. She, who never flirted. But she didn't usually drink champagne either, she realised, panicking slightly as she acknowledged to herself that she wasn't in control—of herself or anything else! She shook her head. 'I think you had better drive me home, Zack,' she told him huskily.

He moved slightly, so that Helen had no choice but to back up against the door-frame, the heat of his body penetrating even the wool of her dress. 'You are home, Helen,' he assured her softly, his eyes so dark now that they appeared almost black.

She swallowed hard, held captive by his very proximity, her breath coming in short gasps. 'But——' Her protest died in her throat as Zack's lips moved the mere inches that separated them from hers, something akin to an electric shock passing through her body at this physical contact with him. She couldn't remember the last time she had been held like this, kissed with this slow, deliberate passion, made to feel desirable...

Her arms moved up about his neck, pulling him down to her, revelling in his exploring lips, tongue gently probing, her body hot and trembling as his hands moved restlessly against her, a low groan sounding in her throat as one of his hands—such beautifully sensual hands, long and tapered, gentle and yet strangely possessive—moved to cup her breast through the thin woollen dress.

Helen's back arched instinctively for closer contact, and as she did so she moved sideways, losing her balance, toppling to the floor, taking Zack with her...!

CHAPTER FOUR

THERE were a dozen little men sitting inside her head with enormous hammers that they kept banging against the side of her skull. Helen didn't know why they were doing it—they just were, and they didn't seem to want to stop.

Her eyelids felt as if they had gravel beneath them as she tried to move them, and they must surely weigh a stone each.

And when she finally did manage to open them enough to look about her, she quickly closed them again!

Where was she?

She opened first one lid, and then the other, moving her gaze suspiciously about the room, knowing exactly where she was now. Zack's bedroom.

Not the bedroom that had been hers when she shared this house with him, but actually *Zack's* bedroom. Not that she had actually had much occasion to enter it when she lived here two years ago, but she did recognise the austere brown and cream décor, the big oak furniture, this king-size bed she now lay in.

Naked, she realised, when she risked a look under the bedclothes. Completely naked.

How had she got here? Who had undressed her? Put her in this bed?

How *long* had she been here? The clock beside the bed said it was ten o'clock, and she knew that had to be in the morning because they hadn't finished their meal until late last night.

She could vaguely recall the evening, the reality of Emily's engagement to Greg, her own feelings of helplessness at that, the champagne—oh, God, the champagne! The rest of the evening was a little hazy after the champagne, although she seemed to recall Zack driving her back home, some confusion about where they actually were, Zack kissing her...

And then what? What happened after Zack kissed her? She couldn't remember!

But she had to, had always pooh-poohed those claims made by people that they had been so affected by drink that they couldn't remember what had happened to them while under the influence of it, had always believed it was an excuse on their part not to be called upon to be responsible for their actions. Until now. She really didn't remember what had happened last night after Zack kissed her!

How awful: she had drunk so much champagne, she had no idea whether or not she and Zack had made love...

She sat up in the bed, burying her face in her hands. This was terrible. Awful. She *had* to remember!

But she couldn't.

But she had to have got here, in Zack's bed, naked, somehow. She looked at the bed beside her, searching for some sign of Zack's having slept next to her. But she had been so sprawled out across the bed when she woke up, it was difficult to tell whether she had disturbed the pillows or whether it had been the indentation of Zack's head there as he lay in the bed with her. In the bed she had never shared with him while they were married...

She should never have met Zack at all, knew that socially they never would have. That could have been because Helen didn't really *have* a social life, although it was improbable that she would have met Zack that way even if she had gone out more. Zack was a senior surgeon at one of London's leading hospitals, and as Helen was a mere assistant to a more than temperamental Latin florist who thought nothing of venting her not inconsiderable temper on the floral displays that adorned the shop—usually by throwing them haphazardly about while claiming she had had enough of England and its coldness, that she was going to give it all up and return to her native sunshine home—Helen and Zack's paths weren't really likely to cross on a professional level either.

Until, that was, Zack's mother telephoned the shop to ask for someone to call and start providing the floral displays in the home she shared with her son and grandson. Zack and Greg.

Helen couldn't even have begun to guess the impact that the Neilson family were going to have on her life as she innocently parked the shop van outside the impressive townhouse that first day. The top three floors were visibly well cared for, and as she went round the back to the service entrance, and was let into the warm, cosy kitchen by the cook-housekeeper, she could see that this part of the house was more than comfortable too.

She had expected to just deliver the displays she had brought with her initially, and then come in on a regular basis to replenish them as the flowers began to wilt and die in the centrally heated home; she had the same arrangement with several other homes in London, the lady of the house either not inclined to do the flowers herself or too busy.

But Barbara Neilson had asked to see her when she arrived, and as soon as Helen saw her she knew that the other woman was different from those others; this once-beautiful woman was already ravaged by illness, despite the fact that her short dark hair, which was liberally sprinkled with grey, was perfectly coiffured, her make-up artfully applied to conceal some of the pain her illness caused her, the peach linen suit and matching blouse obviously designer labels.

She had been warm and gracious, explaining that although she liked to see fresh flowers in the house at all times she now found it too tiring to go out of the house to purchase them, let alone exert the energy it would take to sit and lovingly arrange them as she used to.

Helen had liked the older woman immediately, and there had begun a strong friendship between the two women, the one slowly being defeated by an illness that was slowly debilitating her, the other trying desperately to support herself, her father, and her young daughter by juggling around the tempestuous emotions of a volatile employer.

Helen usually called at the Neilson house twice a week, encouraging Barbara to help out with the flowers on the days she felt strong enough, just chatting to her lightly as she worked on the days Barbara was in too much pain.

Always after she had completed her work Barbara would insist she sit and share a pot of coffee with her, and although Helen knew her employer would be more than a little angry if she knew she was apparently 'wasting' working time she stayed and enjoyed the coffee anyway, knowing that Barbara looked forward to their chats together, that although the older woman had friends who called occasionally she found it more and more difficult to get out herself. It could be a very long, lonely day for Barbara with her son and grandson out of the house all week.

It was inevitable that they should talk on a more personal level than they might otherwise have done, Barbara talking of her extremely clever only child, of how she had come to live with him and Greg when the little boy was only five and his mother had been killed in a car crash, Barbara taking over the running of the household for Zack and looking after Greg so that Zack might continue with his career.

In return Helen had confided her own early marriage and then widowhood at only eighteen when her daughter was still only a baby, of the home she had shared with her father since the death of her mother just before Emily was born. There were a lot of things she didn't tell Barbara about her too-young marriage, her husband's untimely death only a year later, and the years since. But in a way she had always felt Barbara half guessed some of those, that she had become the confidante Helen's mother had never been, that she didn't need to talk of the struggle it still was to keep her family together, of the growing financial demands put upon her as Emily matured, demands that meant she had to tolerate a less-than-easy employer because she needed the money her job provided. Barbara seemed to know all those things without Helen having to talk of them.

And then had come Helen's first meeting with Zack...

Having heard so much about him, Helen was expecting a saint and the Archangel Gabriel all rolled into one. What she got was something else entirely!

He had always been out on the days that Helen called at the house, but this particular day he had apparently taken a day's leave, and Barbara had introduced the two of them with all the confidence of a person who was sure they would like each other.

Zack had treated Helen with hostility, suspicious of her friendship with his mother!

But out of concern for his mother he had shown none of these emotions in her presence, was polite to Helen then, if a little cool. It had only been later, when he supposedly 'walked with her to the door' that he had voiced his mistrust of the friendship.

Helen had felt angry and insulted at the things he said to her, and although she felt guilty about disappointing Barbara she had talked Maria into going to the Neilson house in her place for the next scheduled call, and she certainly hadn't just popped in to see Barbara if she was in the area, as she had started to do!

Maria had returned from the call muttering about 'that disagreeable old woman', telling Helen that she would have to go next time. Such was Helen's upset from her encounter with Zachariah Neilson that for the first time in her life she took a day off sick when she didn't need to, just to avoid making that call to the Neilson house.

When Zack himself called at the shop the next day she had felt like running for cover!

'My mother is concerned she might have done something to upset you,' he informed Helen tautly—both of them knowing it wasn't Barbara who had done that! 'Very concerned,' he added coldly. 'In fact, it is aggravating her condition!'

It seemed she could do nothing right where this man was concerned, that even when she did what he apparently wanted, and stayed away from his mother, that was wrong too!

And so she had resumed calling on Barbara to do the flowers, although she curtailed those other impromptu visits, even though she could see that Barbara was puzzled by the sudden distance she seemed to want to put between them. But each time she went to the house Helen hoped and prayed that Zachariah Neilson wouldn't be there, her nerves jangling until it was confirmed that he wasn't.

As her friendship with Barbara continued, albeit a little strained on Helen's side, her position as Maria's assistant became even more precarious, until it all came to a sudden end one day when Maria just came into the shop and told her she was selling up and going back to Italy to live. Helen was devastated—she had a fifteen-year-old daughter and a seventy-five-year-old father to support, and suddenly, without warning, she was going to be out of work. She had done her rounds in a daze that day, finally spilling out the whole sorry mess to Barbara when the other woman showed her concern at how pale she was.

Barbara's answer to that, without telling Helen she was doing it, was to buy the shop from Maria and put Helen in as her manager!

When Helen had protested at the enormity of what Barbara had done, the other woman treated it all lightly, claiming she was probably their best customer anyway, so she might as well own the shop!

But Helen knew it was so much more than that, that Barbara wouldn't even have thought of investing in a florist's shop if Helen hadn't been someone she had come to care about. And although she had become fond of the older woman too she now felt guilty for involving her in her problems, hadn't meant for Barbara to actually financially involve herself in that way, had just needed a friendly shoulder to cry on. God knew what Zachariah Neilson would have to say if he found out about it! He would no doubt believe it was all Helen's doing, that she had influenced his mother in some devious way!

And so she had refused Barbara's offer, said that she really couldn't accept something of such enormity, no matter how generously it was meant.

She had reckoned without Barbara's stubbornness, had discovered that the older woman had the same streak of determination that smacked of outright arrogance in her son! Barbara had calmly informed her that if she wouldn't run the shop for her then she would employ someone who would, and that she, Helen, would be out of a job anyway! Put like that, it had seemed churlish to continue to refuse, but Helen had insisted that it all be done on a business level, that she had a proper contract of employment.

And for two months the arrangement had worked out ideally for both of them. But Barbara's condition was slowly worsening, the cancer that was slowly claiming most of her body now confining her to her bedroom, although she still managed to leave her bed for a few hours each day. But with her rapidly failing health came an almost obsessive concern for her son and grandson.

Helen was made aware of just how obsessive that concern had become when Zachariah Neilson himself came to see her to ask her to be his wife!

She had simply stared at him after the coldly made request; they didn't even like each other!

And then he had explained that he didn't really want her to marry him—whew!—he only wanted his mother to *believe* she was going to be his wife so that Barbara might die believing that the future of the son she loved, and the young woman she had come to look on as a daughter, was happily settled. Together.

Of course Helen had refused. It was totally unthinkable to find herself engaged to this arrogant man, even for Barbara's sake.

But Zack meant his mother's last weeks to be happy, contented ones, and he wasn't averse to using any method at his disposal to achieve it, first playing on her feelings for Barbara, then on the concern she had for Emily's future by offering to pay for her daughter's education through college and university, and then, ultimately, blackmail, using his mother's ownership of the shop as leverage. Barbara was so ill now that her lawyers had consulted Zack on her business affairs; the florist's shop Helen ran, he had discovered, was one of them. He had left Helen in no doubt as to how he felt about that, or how he believed it had been achieved.

It was exactly the way Helen had feared it might be!

A few weeks, he had told Helen, and then she was free to do what the hell she liked. Go to the devil, probably, his tone had implied.

Helen had been numbed by his bulldozing tactics, hadn't even had time to agonise over it further as Zack took it upon himself to announce their engagement to his mother. Barbara's obvious delight with the news she had so hoped for had convinced Helen it had been the right thing to do, although she deplored Zack's methods in achieving it.

But what neither she, nor, she was sure, Zack, had thought through properly was the effect their engagement would have on the rest of their families. Emily had thought it was wonderful that she was to have a father at last, and even Zack's son Greg had been warmly welcoming of the idea of having Helen as a stepmother; he certainly greeted the idea of having Emily as a stepsister with the greatest enthusiasm, the two of them liking each other at their very first meeting. Helen's father had been another proposition completely; he didn't like Zack, or the idea of her marrying him, in the least, and he made no effort to hide his antagonism.

And Barbara confounded them all by rallying slightly, claiming that it was because she was determined to see Zack and Helen happily married before she died!

Zack had grimly informed Helen that they were to have an Easter wedding. Easter was only three weeks away!

The whole thing—the engagement, the wedding—had been like the momentum of a tiny snowball going down a hill, having grown to gigantic proportions by the time it reached the bottom. 'When first you practise to deceive'; no matter with what good intentions you might believe it was, Helen realised, it was sure to end in disaster. Or being married to Zachariah Neilson!

They were married three weeks later by special licence, in front of his mother and their two children, Helen's father refusing to even attend the ceremony.

The house Helen had grown up in, and continued to share with her father even after her first marriage, had been rented, and five years before Helen even met Barbara she had taken the courageous step of taking out a mortgage herself on that house when the landlord offered it to them to buy. It had either been that or he put it on the open market, and the mortgage payments on the house had only been a little more than the rent they would have had to pay on some of the other houses they looked at. Because her father had refused to move into the Neilson house after she married Zack she had kept up the payments on that house so that he could continue to live there, although she accepted Zack's offer of a housekeeper for him so that he shouldn't be alone. But in spite of that—or maybe because of it?—her father lost no opportunity, when she visited him at the house, to make vitriolic remarks about her 'husband'.

In truth, Zack was far from being that, the two of them having separate bedrooms, even if they were adjoining, something Barbara wasn't aware of because by this time she didn't leave her own bedroom at all. And in front of his mother Zack was charmingly attentive to Helen, giving no hint of the fact that the rest of the time they had as little to do with each other as possible. It seemed that Zack would go to any lengths to please the mother he adored. In fact, Helen lived in dread of Barbara expressing a wish for more grandchildren—*there* she would have drawn the line!

Barbara had lived almost five months after their wedding, had died with the quiet grace with which she had lived. It had been an emotionally traumatic time for all of them, and Zack, despite his medical training and the expectation that his mother wouldn't live much longer, had been hit the hardest.

He had contained his grief behind a wall of efficiency as he carried out all the funeral arrangements himself, and then after the last mourners had departed the house Helen had gone up to Barbara's private sitting-room to find him on his knees on the carpet, apparently having dropped there when emotion overcame him, tears scalding a path down the hardness of his cheeks.

Helen had hesitated only fractionally before going to him, not knowing whether he would simply hate her more for having seen him like this, but at the same time knowing she couldn't just walk away and leave him like that.

She had knelt beside him, cradling him in her arms, his head against her breasts. He resisted at first, torn between pride, and need, the latter winning as his body was racked by deep sobs of overwhelming grief. Helen cried with him; she had come to love Barbara more than ever during the months she had lived in this house as her daughter-in-law.

Zack finally raised his head to look at her, his face ravaged by despair. 'We did the right thing, didn't we?' His thoughts were obviously on the same lines as Helen's. 'We made her happy, didn't we?' he said fiercely.

'Yes,' she answered without hesitation, knowing it was true. 'Yes, we did.' And she was glad. Glad!

Zack's hands moved to grip the tops of her arms painfully. 'I would do it all again, you know.'

Helen knew exactly what he was saying to her, knew that he didn't, and never would, offer any apology for having forced her into marrying him. At the time Helen had hated him for the pressure he had exerted to achieve his objective, but she had only to think of the happiness and contentment on Barbara's face shortly before she died to know that it had been the right thing to do. The tangled web left by her death would have to be dealt with as efficiently.

'Helen?' Zack shook her slightly, his eyes darkening as she looked up at him with warmth and compassion. 'Helen...!' he groaned before his mouth came crashing down on hers. Compassion was the last emotion he wanted from her.

Her own emotions were too raw, their senses heightened, desire quickly raging out of control, Zack's lips devouring as they moved heatedly over hers, his need to possess in the throbbing heat of his body.

Helen pulled back. 'Zack, we can't,' she gasped. 'Not here!' She groaned at the impossibility of it all.

His answer to that was to lay her back against the cream-coloured carpet, holding her gaze with the darkness of his as he slowly unfastened the buttons on the black dress she had worn to the funeral only hours ago, pushing the sombre material aside, revealing the lacy cream underwear she wore beneath it.

He ran an insistent hand down the length of her body, her clothes discarded as if by magic, his own along with them, until he lay next to her like a magnificently beautiful sculpture, all hard planes and smooth golden skin, a silky covering of dark hair over the whole of his body, thickening as it reached the base of his stomach and thighs. Here Helen's gaze stopped, returning shyly to his face.

Zack inhaled sharply, his eyes black as he lay the length of his body against hers, hungry lips moving down her throat, and then lower, their moistness hovering for a mindless second above her arching breast, before his head swooped and he sucked a warm, already erect nipple into the deep, warm cavern of his mouth. As his tongue stroked wetly against the hardened nub, hot desire fired the rest of her body, her arms about his neck straining him closer to her as the hardness of him moved restlessly against her damp thighs.

'Please, Zack,' she gasped her need. 'Please!'

'It's too soon,' he groaned with a shake of his head before turning his attention to her other breast, the pleasure exquisite torture now as this received the same loving caress.

It seemed the most natural thing in the world for his hand to caress the silkiness of her flesh down to her thighs, lingering there, finding the very centre of her desire, finding her moist and hot and oh, so ready for him.

If he didn't take her soon she was going to simply explode!

As his body moved to cover hers and he entered her with gentle possession, pausing to allow her to become familiar with the feel of him inside her, Helen thought she was going to explode anyway!

Tiny little spasms of pleasure were bursting inside her and threatening to engulf her completely, Zack fitting perfectly inside her, his own control fast slipping away as the hardness of him shuddered his need to move and caress.

Helen wrapped the length of her legs about his hips, pulling him even closer into her, moving restlessly against him.

Zack raised his head to look down into her flushed face, at the pouting sensuality of her mouth where his lips had claimed hers, the burning longing in over-bright grey eyes, and what he saw there reassured him as he at last began to move inside her, slowly at first, the thrusts becoming more and more urgent as liquid fire pulsed through her veins, the pleasure such now that it was out of control, *she* was out of control, crying out her pleasure as spasm after spasm of pure delight took her up high on to that plateau of ecstasy. And as she tumbled down over the other side she felt Zack explode moistly inside her, heard his own cries of fulfilment, and exulted in the knowledge that she had been the one to take him there, crying with the sheer beauty of being made love to by him.

The clarity of that memory was always with her, because it had been the first and last time Zack had ever made love to her.

Except, perhaps, for last night . . . ?

She looked up with a start of surprise as the bedroom door swung open now without warning, didn't even have time to pull the sheet up over her nakedness before Zack entered the room, his warm gaze moving mockingly over her flushed face. Almost as if he was able to guess at the intimacy of her thoughts seconds ago. But he couldn't. Of course he couldn't!

'Good morning,' he greeted her drily, carrying a tray over to the side of the bed with the orange juice, coffee, and toast that he knew was all she liked for breakfast in the morning. At least he had remembered that about her, hadn't obliterated everything from his mind about the woman he had made his second wife!

'Good morning!' she returned the greeting disgustedly as she held the sheet to her defensively, even the smell of the food on the tray making her feel ill as Zack put it down on the bedside table. She *had* been drunk last night, couldn't bring herself to apologise to this man for her behaviour, but knew she would have to make some sort of explanation to Emily and Greg when she saw them at the party tonight. Although the last thing she felt like doing was going to the party at all; *she* was the one who now blanched at the thought of the loud music!

'Hm.' Zack crossed the room confidently to draw back the curtains, and the sun, as if to prove his statement, streamed in through the window. His brow was raised slightly in query as he turned back to find her watching him with searching intensity.

Had she made love with this man last night? Had she lain naked in his arms, caressed the hard beauty of his body? Oh, God, just thinking about it made her feel hot and cold at the same time!

Zack's mouth twisted with humour as he seemed able to read her chaotic thoughts, crossing the room to sit on the edge of the bed next to her. 'Sleep well?'

Helen swallowed hard. Had she slept well? She didn't even know that; it was all just a blank to her after she had kissed him on the doorstep!

His hand moved, long fingers caressing the heat of her cheeks. 'You were sleeping like the proverbial baby when I left you in bed this morning,' he told her huskily.

Oh, God, he *had* shared this bed with her last night! And the hard possession in his eyes as he looked down at her told her they hadn't slept all the time either.

She didn't understand it; that other memory she had of making love with Zack was all too vivid, and yet she didn't even remember being in this bed with him, let alone anything else that might have happened! Her mouth twisted in confusion.

'Something amusing you?' Zack's head tilted in quizzical query, his thumb moving against her bottom lip now.

Amusing? It was all so funny she wanted to—*cry*!

Instead she fell back on her defences, turning her head away from that caressing hand, his touch having the strangest effect on her lower limbs, the sudden heat between her thighs making her shift uncomfortably, her nipples hard and erect beneath the sheet that hid them from the warmth of Zack's gaze.

'You must be losing your touch, Zack,' she taunted, wishing to God she sounded more convincing! 'Last night was distinctly un-memorable.'

Instead of the anger she had been hoping for Zack just looked more mocking, making no effort to move off the side of the bed, jean-clad thigh so dangerously close, pinning her beneath the sheet. 'Perhaps you just need your memory jogging...?' His head dipped slowly towards her, and Helen gazed up at him in dazed fascination as his intention to kiss her became more and more obvious.

Almost at the last second, his lips only fractions of an inch away from claiming hers, a pulse beating a wild tattoo in her throat at the pleasure she knew that mouth offered, Helen pulled away, shifting quickly over to the other side of the bed—the side he had slept on last night?—desperately looking around for something she could pull over her nakedness so that she might escape to the adjoining bathroom; duvets might be the most practical and easy things to have on beds nowadays, but she certainly couldn't wrap a cumbersome thing like that around her and rush off to the bathroom!

Zack stood up slowly, seemingly unconcerned that she had evaded his kiss, stretching languidly now, pulling the cream-coloured shirt he wore taut across the width of his shoulders, before strolling over to the floor-to-ceiling wardrobe that covered one wall of the bedroom.

He looked casually through the contents. 'Here!' He turned to throw something at her.

Helen reacted instinctively, reaching out to catch the silky article he tossed over to her so casually, and dropped the sheet that covered her as she did so, instantly baring rosy-tipped breasts to his appreciative gaze.

She turned away with a defiant lift of her chin; she was thirty-five years old, had made love with this man—if not last night, then definitely two years ago!—she couldn't now start behaving like a gauche teenager, too shy to show her naked body. Even if that was how Zack made her feel!

Her shoulders drooped dejectedly at the thought of last night—she should *know* if she had made love with Zack then!

He had thrown her one of his white evening shirts, silkily soft against her skin as she pulled it on.

Zack stood across the room watching her every move as she buttoned it up, her fingers shaking slightly at the dark caress in that gaze. As she stood up the shirt barely reached her thighs, her bare legs long and golden beneath its short length. And although she determinedly didn't look at Zack she knew he was still watching her, could feel the heat of his stare.

'I telephoned your father and told him you were safe and well,' he spoke softly.

Now Helen did look at him, her head snapping back as if she had been struck. Her father! Oh, God, she hadn't given him another thought, not this morning, and certainly not last night. Her head began to pound again, and she put up a hand to her throbbing temple.

'Headache?' Zack drawled drily. 'I have something in the bathroom you can take.'

He was her headache, Helen decided irritably as she could hear him searching through the contents of the cabinet in the adjoining bathroom. Not only did the two of them know she had spent the night here with him, but now her father knew it too; she might have got away with telling him she had stayed the night at Emily's flat if Zack hadn't interfered, and just had to apologise for her thoughtlessness in not calling him and letting him know. Of course, it was ridiculous that she had to explain herself at all, but she had lived with her father for so long now that it had become second nature to her. And she had never stayed out all night before!

Zack came back with the promised medication and a glass of water to take it with, standing over her as she swallowed the tablets.

She must look awful, knew she must, still had her make-up on from last night, her hair was probably standing up on end, and——

'You look beautiful,' Zack spoke softly above her bent head.

How had he known——? Helen gave him a startled look. A hazy memory was coming back to her, something to do with him having said that before...?

She remembered. Last night. Before—— No, she couldn't think of that, had to concentrate on here and now!

She held out the empty glass for Zack to take. 'When did you telephone my father?' she prompted wearily.

He raised dark brows, shrugging. 'Last night. I knew you wouldn't want him to worry,' he added derisively, emphasising the fact that as far as he personally was concerned he didn't care whether her father worried or not!

That meant her father had had all night to brood on his condemnation of her, and his years in the Royal Air Force meant that he could rip a person to shreds without even raising his voice. A perfect end to a less-than-perfect night!

Zack watched the emotions flickering across her face. 'You're a big girl now, Helen,' he reminded her gently.

It wasn't a question of maturity when it came to her father, she just wanted to keep their life as quietly untroubled as possible, always had to consider the fact that her father took medication for his heart complaint. She wondered whether or not he had remembered to take his pills today without her there to remind him.

Her face took on a hunted look. 'I have to go, Zack,' she told him distractedly. 'If you could just tell me where my clothes are...' Her voice trailed off as she *saw* where her clothes were as she stepped past him: scattered all over the bedroom floor!

And she didn't even want to think how they had got there, hurriedly picking up the blue dress and the skimpy bits of lace that were her bra and panties, the latter still tangled up with the dark sheer tights.

Zack was standing incredibly close to her when she straightened, and her cheeks flushed as the warmth of his breath softly ruffled the hair at her temple.

Helen gave a strained squeak, rushing towards the sanctuary of the bathroom.

His mocking voice followed her. 'After last night, divorce between us is out of the question...'

CHAPTER FIVE

HELEN tripped over the dress as it trailed down in front of her when she spun back round to face Zack, steadying herself with a hand on the dressing-table. 'What did you say?' She couldn't have heard him correctly, he couldn't *really* have said he was no longer agreeable to the divorce.

His hands were thrust into the pockets of his denims, the shrug he gave her completely dismissive. 'We aren't getting divorced in September,' he told her drily.

He *had* said that! But he couldn't be serious. This had to be just his warped idea of a joke.

The same way she had thought Emily and Greg's engagement announcement was a joke...?

But that was different, she mentally chided herself; their children weren't married yet, and they never would be if she had her way, whereas she and Zack were married, and she, at least, no longer wanted to be. God, she had served her time; two years as Zack's wife was long enough for anybody!

'Because we spent the night together?' she protested disbelievingly. 'I can't believe——'

'Helen, memorable as last night between *us* was,' he cut in derisively, 'I was talking about our children's engagement!'

Really, she was going to have this high colour permanently in her cheeks whenever she was near this man if she didn't learn to control her blushes! But she felt such a fool, had made the assumption that when he referred to 'last night' he had been talking about them, here together, in his bed. Only to be very firmly put in her place by Zack!

What had she thought he meant? They had made love once before, and it had made no difference to her leaving, permanently, once a decent interval had elapsed after Barbara's death. Zack certainly hadn't tried to stop her going because they had made love, and last night made no difference to their decision to divorce either. She didn't happen to think that Emily and Greg's engagement should affect it either.

'Of course you were,' she answered Zack tautly, deliberately not meeting the mockery that she knew would be in his gaze. 'But I happen to believe that the sooner we are divorced and the connection between our two families is finally severed, the more chance there is that Emily and Greg will realise they have made a mistake too.'

'I don't agree with you,' Zack rasped. 'They——'

'I didn't for one moment believe you would.' She shook her head disgustedly. 'You never have before, so why start now?' She sighed her impatience.

'Look, Helen, I don't—— Will you go and get some clothes on?' he suddenly rasped harshly. 'We can't conduct this conversation sensibly with you dressed—or *un*dressed—like that.' His eyes were narrowed critically.

'I'm sure you've had "conversations" with women wearing less than this!' she scorned, knowing damn well that he had. They might have been married, but that hadn't stopped Zack from carrying on with his very private life exactly as he had before she came along, discreetly enough for Barbara not to be aware of it, of course. But Helen had known.

'Not with my wife!' he bit out tautly.

Helen bit back the angry retort she had been about to make about 'someone else's wife' as she saw how tightly his jaw was clenched, a nerve pulsing in the deep groove of his cheek. Good God, Zack was actually physically affected by her nakedness beneath the silk of his shirt. Superman, for all his mockery of her, had a chink in his own armour; he was human after all!

And then she realised how unfair she was being to him; it had been because of the love he had for his mother that he had forced their marriage at all. Zack had sacrificed as much for the marriage as she had—— No, he hadn't, damn it, she warred with herself. Life for Zack had carried on pretty much as it had before they were married; Helen was the one whose life had been turned upside-down and inside out. As it still was!

'Only someone else's!' She defiantly issued the angry challenge she had fought back earlier, before going into the bathroom and slamming the door in his face before he could recover enough from the shock of her taunt to make any cutting reply.

She leaned back against the door, breathing hard, could still feel his presence on the other side of the closed door, aware of him with every nerve-ending. It was long, agonising seconds before she heard him move across the bedroom, the soft click of the door as he left and went downstairs, and the breath left her body in a deep sigh of relief as she heard his feet on the stairs. The sooner she was dressed and away from here, the better!

A shower did little to refresh her flagging spirits, the whole of her body seeming to ache, although it was centred around her stomach, where it was obvious that she had drunk too much wine.

Once she had dressed, the full force of just what had happened the night before hit her. And she didn't mean what had taken place here, between herself and Zack, but what had led up to that time. One look at her reflection in the mirror, in the blue clinging dress, her curves emphasised as they had been last night, and she knew that she had deliberately set out to show Zack that she was an attractive woman. God, had she shown him!

Had she wanted him to make love to her? *No*, she knew she hadn't expected that; she had just wanted him to realise that she was a desirable woman. *Why*? She didn't know any more. God, how she hated 'confused' women, and now she had become one!

Zack was in the drawing-room when she eventually went downstairs—it had to be done so she might as well get it over with!—enjoying a cup of coffee from the pot that stood on the low table.

Helen stood in the doorway, watching him unobserved for a few seconds, wondering if he would demand an explanation for her parting shot upstairs; the last thing she wanted was to get into recriminations for the past, recriminations she had no right to feel.

Zack turned and saw her, as if sensing her presence there, his mocking gaze on the tray she had brought down with her, the toast and orange juice untouched. 'Just put it down on the table,' he dismissed. 'Mrs Grey will clear it away later with these other things. There's fresh coffee in the pot.' He scorned the fact that she *had* drunk the cup of coffee he had brought up on the tray.

'No, thank you.' Helen clasped her hands awkwardly together in front of her once she had put the tray down. If this was how it felt to leave in the morning after spending the night with a man—uncomfortable and more than slightly embarrassing—then it was something she wasn't about to make a habit of!

The truth of the matter was that she had only ever had two lovers in all of her thirty-five years, had in fact only made love once with Ian before they were married, and that one time together had been a hurried, fumbling affair because she was expected home by ten-thirty and they had been to the cinema during the evening too. That one unsatisfactory coming together of two inexperienced teenagers had resulted in Emily.

Ian had only been seventeen himself, but once Helen's father had got together with Ian's parents over the pregnancy the two young people were given little choice but to marry. It was either marry Ian or have an abortion, those were her father's choices, since he was not prepared to have the respectability that he valued so highly dragged down, as he saw it, because of an illegitimate grandchild.

Her poor mother had been on the verge of a nervous breakdown because of her husband's vow that if Helen didn't marry Ian he would throw her out of the house and they never wanted to see her again.

Helen knew that she should have been strong, should have left home and had her baby alone, as she had wanted to do. Instead she had given in to family pressure and married Ian.

The marriage had been a disaster from the first, the young couple moving in with Helen's parents after the wedding, supposedly just until they could afford somewhere of their own. But when Helen was in her sixth month of pregnancy her mother had unexpectedly died of a heart attack, and after that there was no question, in her father's mind at least, of their moving out and leaving him to live alone. And at the back of Helen's mind she hadn't been altogether sure that it hadn't been the strain over her pregnancy that had brought on the attack . . .

Ian had hated their living arrangements, had begun to stay out as much as possible, even more so after Emily was born, begun to drink heavily too. The physical side of their marriage, never very exciting for Helen at best, a duty to be performed at worst, was never resumed after Emily was born, the two of them living more like brother and sister than husband and wife.

Ian was three times over the alcohol limit when he drove his motorbike into the side of a car and was killed outright.

It had been difficult, when Emily was a baby, for Helen to keep up the friendships with the girls she had been at school with, for she had little in common with them any more, since she had become a wife, mother and widow, all within the space of a single year. And so she had brought Emily up and kept house for her father, and when Emily started school she found herself a part-time job, and then as Emily got older she began to work full time, all the time making a home for her father too.

She was still a young woman, but she had no social life to speak of, her life revolving around Emily and her father, no qualifications either except the natural flair she seemed to have with floral arrangements, a flair that secured her employment at least. On a social level she shied away from becoming involved in a relationship.

There had been no other man in her life until Zack. And that time with him, two years ago, was the only other time she had ever made love with a man...

Making love with Zack was nothing like being with Ian, Zack's gentleness and care, his experience, making it a totally satisfying time for both of them. It had been beautiful, a memory she allowed to sustain her whenever she was in danger of letting things become too much for her.

Two years ago she had realised that she was in love with Zack, with the way he could make her feel with his lips and his hands—but once he had come to his senses he had made it plain that he regretted ever coming near her, let alone taking their relationship on to an intimate level.

She stiffened her shoulders defensively now as she looked across the room at him. 'I have to go.'

Zack's gaze narrowed questioningly on the paleness of her cheeks. 'We haven't finished our conversation,' he reminded her slowly.

She shook her head. 'I'm not up to this just now.' Whatever he had given her for her headache had done little to ease the ache in her stomach!

His mouth twisted. 'When do you think you will be "up to it"?' he derided hardly.

There was nothing in this stony-faced man to show that a short time ago in the bedroom upstairs he had been totally aware of her as a woman; he was completely in control again now, infuriatingly so when she still felt so aware of a sense of awkwardness in having to put on the clothes she had worn the evening before!

'There's nothing more for us to discuss,' she told him with abrupt dismissal. 'I will talk to Emily about how impossible it is for them to marry in September, and I trust you will do the same with Greg——'

'Oh, I'll talk to him—for all the good it will do me,' Zack said scornfully.

She frowned at his attitude. 'Greg is your son——'

'Exactly,' he acknowledged pointedly. 'I didn't listen to my parents when they advised against my marrying so young, and I doubt Greg will listen to me either! Financially,' he added firmly as Helen would have protested at that belief; Greg respected his father's opinion very much, 'even if I did withdraw my support, Greg has a small monthly allowance from my mother that would ensure he and Emily didn't starve. Besides,' Zack concluded softly, 'I don't actually disapprove of the two of them wanting to get married.'

Helen gasped. 'But—but——'

'They're good together, haven't you noticed?' He gave an indulgent smile at the thought of their two children together.

She had noticed how perfectly Emily and Greg sparked off each other, and it had only added to her dismay about the whole business. She was very aware of the fact that it was because of her that the two youngsters had met at all!

'They're too young, Zack——'

'Of course they're too young,' he accepted harshly, his indulgence fading as impatience took over. 'When I said I don't disapprove of their getting married, I meant at some time in the future, not now. But legally, I'm aware, we can't stop them if they decide to go ahead and get married without our approval. And the pair of them are just stubborn enough to go ahead and do it!' he added grimly. 'Which is why I'm no longer agreeable to our divorce.'

Helen frowned, shaking her head in puzzlement. 'Zack, you aren't making sense; why should our postponing our divorce make any difference to when Emily and Greg get married?'

He shrugged. 'Something along the lines of ''united we stand, divided we fall''?'

She vaguely recalled having thoughts something like that herself last night, but even so... 'You've never ''fallen'', Zack,' she scorned.

He regarded her with an unfathomable expression in his eyes. 'Haven't I?' he finally said softly. 'Divorce is a form of failure.'

'That's ridiculous,' she flashed, her cheeks flushed. 'We were never really married!'

Zack shook his head. 'I knew exactly what I was doing when I married you.'

'So did I,' she scoffed; Zack had been ensuring that his mother's last months were happy ones—and carrying on his own life exactly as before in private! 'I'm going ahead with an application for our divorce in September, Zack,' she told him stubbornly.

'Why?' He frowned at her determination. 'Is there someone else in your life?'

'No,' she answered instantly; but there had always been someone else in his!

His eyes narrowed, dark as coal. 'Apply all you want, Helen, but I won't agree to it.'

She glared at him frustratedly. 'You're being ridiculous! Our not going through with the divorce just yet won't make the slightest difference to Emily and Greg's plans.' In fact, it might have the opposite effect, give their children the idea that they might be trying to salvage their marriage, that marriage itself was worth achieving.

'Why the hell do you think they want to get married at this young age in the first place?' Zack challenged angrily, every line of his body taut with emotion. 'It's often children from broken homes who——'

'Greg and Emily don't come from broken homes,' she protested indignantly. 'Our respective partners both died.'

'And the two of us, years later, for whatever reason, married each other and provided them with a family unit——'

'It didn't even last for five months, Zack!' she denied, incredulous that he could even think that that had any bearing on this situation.

His expression was grim. 'It was obviously long enough for them to have decided they want to continue living together,' he pointed out firmly.

Her eyes widened. 'I hope you aren't suggesting we all move back into your house and hope Emily and Greg change their mind about getting married?' Helen gasped protestingly. 'Because if you are——'

'I'm not,' Zack cut in harshly. 'I'm just suggesting that maybe if they didn't feel the severing of all family ties looming in the immediate future perhaps they might be persuaded to delay their wedding plans for a while. And once this initial sense of immediacy has worn off we may be able to talk them into a much longer engagement.'

Why was it that this man could make even the most illogical ideas, as far as she was concerned, seem to make sense? It had been the same over Barbara's heartfelt desire to see the two of them married to each other; it had seemed the most sensible and right thing to do once Zack had explained it to her!

But just look how that sensible and right thing had rebounded on them all now! Barbara might have died happy in the knowledge of their marriage, but they were all paying for it now with Emily and Greg's engagement.

Helen gave a firm shake of her head. 'I don't agree with you, Zack——'

'You don't have to,' he rasped dismissively. 'After only two years' separation, I still have to agree with your application for a divorce, and I no longer intend doing so, which should delay things for a while. Now,' he added briskly, the conversation over as far as he was concerned, 'I suggest I drive you to the restaurant so that you can pick up your car. You left it there last night, remember?' he taunted as she looked completely blank.

She hadn't, but she did now, with sickening clarity, those little men starting to bang those hammers inside her head again as she recalled the fact that she had been incapable of driving the night before and that was why her car was still parked at the restaurant!

CHAPTER SIX

'You spent the night with that man, Helen,' her father accused disgustedly. 'I just can't believe it!'

Zack had driven her back to the restaurant earlier, in stony silence, to pick up her car after she had told him she could easily call a taxi and he had refused even to think about it, his cold anger with her turning to burning fury when she had once again offered to reimburse him for the meal she should have paid for last night.

He hadn't even seemed to hear her stilted thanks for giving her a lift to her car, his face tight with icy disgust.

And after driving herself home in her own car, every part of her seeming to ache now, she had to face her father's condemnation. Expected as it was, it was still too much!

'I suppose if it had been any other man you wouldn't have minded!' she flared, angry at being taken to task in this way as if she were a child. Just because she had never chosen to stay out all night before, it didn't mean she didn't have the right to do so if she wished!

Her father drew himself up to his full impressive height, still incredibly slim and fit for a man of his age, having retained the weight of his youth. 'I would mind at any time that my daughter is behaving no better than a——'

'Zack is still my husband, Dad,' she reminded him in a carefully controlled voice before he could actually use that word that would send her completely over the top.

She was going to be sick in a minute!

'Only just,' he accused, undaunted. 'Another few months and——'

'I don't want to talk about it,' she told him with stiff dignity.

She was going to scream in a minute!

'The same way you didn't want to talk about it when you found out that man——'

'He has a name!' She glared, two bright spots of anger in her otherwise pale cheeks.

'Found out that Neilson,' her father amended pointedly, 'had been having an affair with a married woman all the time *you* and he were living together as man and wife!'

His breath was coming in angry, emotional gasps, and there was a livid flush to the rugged hardness of his face.

Helen's indignant anger deflated like a burst balloon; she wished she had never told her father about the other woman in Zack's life.

She had been married to Zack for almost two months when she'd discovered the reason his mother had been so anxious to see him settle down with a wife—of his own! It had been because the woman he had been in love with for years was someone else's wife!

Barbara had confided that to her one day when Helen had sat and read to her for a while after supper; the older woman was absolutely thrilled with the apparent success of her matchmaking between Zack and Helen.

'He was simply wasting his life waiting for Olivia to leave her husband.' Barbara frowned with the effort it took her to talk at all these days. 'She'll never leave her husband.' She shook her head knowingly, the iron-grey hair still as perfectly coiffured, Barbara's hairdresser calling at the house twice a week now, her make-up still painstakingly applied each morning, although her face was ravaged by the illness now.

Helen listened to it all as if in a dream; Zack was in love with another woman, a woman married to someone else!

'Of course it's commendable that Olivia has stayed with her husband all these years since he had the accident,' Barbara continued dismissively, completely unaware of the bombshell she had just dropped on Helen; she probably believed that Zack had confided the affair to his new wife! 'But there was no future in that relationship for Zack. There never was, really. And that romantic love of putting a woman on a pedestal isn't going to keep him warm at night,' she added roguishly. 'Or keep him company in his old age.' She frowned as she obviously thought of her own young widowhood and all the years she had spent since without remarrying. An attractive woman, she must have had her opportunities to do just that, but had chosen not to do so. She obviously didn't want the same fate for Zack.

Helen's movements were perfectly controlled as she carefully folded the newspaper into four and put it to one side. 'I-it's very hard for—Olivia, though.' How she kept her voice level, she didn't know. Zack was in love with a *married woman*; that was why he had never remarried! Incredible. She had thought the only things her husband loved were his family and his work, and not always necessarily in that order! Now she began to wonder if Zack *was* actually at the hospital working all the hours he claimed he was.

Barbara made a scoffing sound. 'I think she's rather enjoyed her position as the bravely-smiling-through wife all these years,' she dismissed sceptically. 'She's certainly managed to keep Zack dangling on a piece of string with this claim of duty to stand by her crippled husband. I can't tell you how relieved I am that Zack fell in love with you.' She smiled at Helen warmly. 'I've despaired of him all these years, I really have.'

And Zack, a man who was decisive to the point of cruelty at times, must have suffered the frustrations of hell at loving a woman who felt duty-bound to remain with a crippled husband who needed her!

And Helen, who had been falling in love with the man she had married, now felt the same frustration over him . . .

But she should never, in a moment of utter despair after leaving Barbara that day, have confided Zack's secret love to her father! She knew that her father hadn't meant to do it, but once he knew about Olivia in Zack's life he had lost no opportunity in encouraging her to end the futility of being with Zack. He hadn't known it was always a marriage of convenience, that she had no right to protest or complain at any of Zack's friendships.

Just as no one had ever guessed how hurt she was to know of Olivia's presence in Zack's life, of the love she had for him herself . . .

She would never have made love to him the day of his mother's funeral if she hadn't loved him. She had exulted in the knowledge that she had been the one who was there for him when he needed someone to hold. But ultimately, when he had still let the marriage end the way he had, she had to accept that it was still Olivia he loved.

Obviously the fact that Olivia was still unattainable to him now was another one of the reasons why he wasn't particularly concerned about ending *their* marriage with the finality of a divorce.

'And what are we going to do about Emily's engagement to his son?' Helen's father challenged suddenly. 'Oh, yes, Helen, I know about that too,' he mocked harshly at the consternation on her face. 'Several people have telephoned here this morning to offer their *congratulations*.' His mouth twisted with distaste.

She put a hand up to her aching temple. 'Greg is Emily's choice——'

'And what if he turns out to be as feckless as his father?'

'Zack isn't feckless!' Helen instantly defended.

'Having an affair with a married woman when you've just married yourself is the action of a loyal and responsible man, I suppose?' her father scorned.

Dark grey eyes flashed a warning at this persistent prodding of a wound that had never really healed. 'I suppose you've always lived such a blameless life, haven't you?' she accused angrily, forgetting caution in her deep agitation. 'Edward Jackson, the paragon of virtue!' Even as she almost shouted the taunt at him she regretted doing it, groaning her dismay as he went white. 'Oh, Daddy, I'm sorry,' she groaned in self-recrimination, making a move towards him.

'No—don't come near me!' He held up a restraining hand. 'One night in that man's bed and you have become a raging shrew.' His back was ramrod-stiff with indignation. 'I'm not sure I recognise you any more.'

Or that he wanted to, she realised with an inward wince. He was right, she *was* behaving like a shrew, and the two of them arguing over this wasn't going to make the situation any easier to sort out.

She drew in a steadying breath. 'As it happens, both Zack and I agree with you about Emily and Greg getting engaged——'

'Oh, you did find time last night to actually talk about the subject, then?' her father taunted.

'Dad—please.' She looked at him imploringly, sighing deeply when she received no answering softening of his sternly disapproving expression. 'We're trying, without running the risk of antagonising them and so completely alienating them against listening to any reasoning, to get them to take their time over making any immediate plans as regards marriage.'

'Just forbid it,' her father snapped incredulously. 'That's the way I would deal with it.'

Yes, he would, Helen realised wearily; it was the way he had always dealt with things. And if he trampled over people along the way to do it then his attitude was that they shouldn't have got in his way in the first place. But Emily was far from being the compliant teenager that Helen had been; her daughter had a definite mind of her own!

She shook her head. 'They are both over the age of consent now. We can only persuade, we can't order.' Although she was sure Zack would have liked to!

Her father's mouth tightened. 'I know what I would like to do with the young——'

'Emily *wants* to marry Greg,' Helen reasoned irritably.

'*She's* too young to know what she wants,' he dismissed in clipped tones.

'I was already married and a mother at her age,' Helen reminded him with a sigh.

'Exactly!' her father pounced triumphantly. 'And look what a mess that turned out to be. Another disaster!'

Helen had to bite her tongue to stop herself from reminding him that *he* had been the one to insist she marry Ian at the time, that by the time they had realised Emily was on the way Helen and Ian had also known their relationship was a mistake. But by then, with her father's insistent behaviour, it had been too late to do anything but compound the mistake by marrying each other and being completely unhappy!

Her father had never seen it that way, or else he had chosen to forget it over the years. Just as he wasn't really listening to what she had to say now... There was no reasoning with him over Emily and Greg's engagement, so she might just as well save her breath. She felt too ill to continue just now anyway.

'I'll have to go and lie down, Dad,' she told him now, her face wan. 'I need to feel a lot better than I do now if I'm to get through Emily's party tonight.' But she would definitely stay away from champagne tonight. And every other night too, if that was the effect it was going to have on her!

Her father's eyes narrowed. 'Is Neilson going to be at that one too?'

She hadn't actually thought about it, but she supposed, in the light of the engagement, that it was a distinct possibility. 'He could be,' she acknowledged cautiously with a frown.

'In that case, I think I'll come too,' her father decided firmly.

Helen stared at him with widely indignant eyes. The reason they had arranged for the two completely separate evenings in the first place had been so that her father could go to the quiet dinner party and help celebrate Emily's birthday, since he had informed them when they first began discussing Emily's eighteenth birthday that he refused to be present at any loud, noisy party they might plan. And now, just because he had been too stubborn to go to the dinner last night, and because he believed Zack would be there tonight, he was prepared to go to the 'noisy shindig', as he had called tonight's party, after all!

She was going to scream *and* be sick! Any minute!

'Please yourself, Dad,' she told him wearily. 'But I want you to realise now that I can't leave in the middle of the evening to drive you home if you decide the loud music and chatter is too much for you,' she added warningly, feeling too ill now to even stand and reason with him.

'I'll cope,' he told her abruptly. 'And if I decide otherwise there's always a taxi.'

And if it came to that she would never be allowed to hear the end of it! Oh, God, thirty hours ago she had been completely innocent of the complete confusion that was going to take over her life, not least of that being the reaction she still had towards Zack. She was still in love with her husband; it was only the fact that she wasn't having to see him every day that had made that fact bearable to live with. Because it was still a futile love. Zack still had the beautiful Olivia hovering around in the background of his life, probably always would have. And last night—oh, God, last night . . .!

'I'll see you later, Dad,' she managed to excuse herself before hurrying away, only just making it to the bathroom upstairs to be sick. She didn't know if it was the unaccustomed champagne, something she had eaten at the restaurant last night—she could hazard a guess as to what Zack would say it was down to!—but she really did feel very ill now. She was deathly white once she had finished being sick, beads of perspiration standing out on her brow, a pain seeming to have centralised itself over her stomach.

'You look awful,' was her father's comment when she emerged from the bathroom a few minutes later.

She had washed her face in cold water, and felt a little fresher if nothing else. Trust her father to be brutally honest about the way she looked!

'You should have explained that you were going to bed because you didn't feel well,' he added accusingly.

Instead of the assumption he had made: that she was so exhausted after a night in Zack's bed that she needed to get to her own bed for some sleep!

But she very much doubted that explaining to her father would have made any difference to the way he had been with her since she got home. 'It really doesn't matter, Dad.' She shook her head dismissively. 'I'll probably feel a lot better once I've had some sleep.' She saw his disapproval returning as he thought of the sleepless night she had apparently spent in Zack's arms. It certainly hadn't been sleepless; she just wished she could remember enough about it to be able to defend herself!

Her stomach kept churning round even once she had lain down, falling into a restless sleep, waking only to make another frantic dash to the bathroom to be sick again, a feat not all that easily accomplished, the pain having moved to her side now.

She managed to stagger back to the bed, falling into a deeper sleep this time.

Only to be woken up again, what seemed like seconds later, by having a pin-point of light shone into her eyes! First in one eye, and then the other. What on earth——?

She fought through the layers of sleep, trying to focus, but that bright point of light kept blinding her. And then she saw him. Zack!

'What are you doing?' She pushed his hand away from in front of her face, immediately eliminating the light, and struggling into a sitting position.

'You have a nerve coming here, Neilson!' Her father stood beside the bed, glaring down at Zack as he sat on the edge of the bed beside Helen. 'Pushing your way in——'

'You said Helen was ill,' Zack rasped harshly. 'Of course I came.'

'Why the sudden concern, Neilson?' Helen's father scorned. 'Helen has occasionally been unwell during the last two years, and I don't seem to recall your rushing to her bedside then,' he derided knowingly.

She had just woken up, she didn't need this, even if she had actually been asleep for hours, according to her bedside clock! What *was* Zack doing here?

He stood up now, the two men glaring at each other, one so tall and powerful, the other as stubbornly determined, despite his years. 'If I had been informed of her illness then I probably would have done!' Zack snapped.

Her father's mouth twisted with derision. 'I don't believe any of us thought you *cared*!'

White-hot anger burned in Zack's eyes at the taunt, his eyes as black as coal, livid colour across his high cheekbones. 'Now listen here, Edward, I've held my peace all these years where you're concerned——'

'Don't feel you have to do me any favours!' her father put in furiously.

'Because of Helen,' Zack finished pointedly, sparing the older man none of his contempt. 'But don't think I'm going to continue doing so indefinitely,' he grated harshly.

'Personally, I think you're a trouble-making, interfering, manipulative——'

'Old man,' Edward put in scornfully. 'Men like you always belittle by using weapons like that against people.'

Zack's eyes were narrowed to black slits now. 'I wasn't even going to mention your age. Because I don't think age has anything to do with the way you are; I think you've always been the things I called you!'

This was going to result in an out and out slanging match if Helen didn't intervene soon. And while the two men looked as if they might actually enjoy that—the confrontation was probably long overdue—Helen knew that she wasn't up to that just now!

'Excuse me?'

She could almost have laughed at Zack's slightly stunned expression at being reminded of her presence in the room at all! Almost. If it hadn't been for the way her father turned sharply to glare at her. So much for trying to be the peace-maker!

'I can see my presence here is superfluous to both of you,' her father said with stiff dignity. 'I will go downstairs and make you a cup of tea, Helen.'

She grimaced ruefully up at Zack as her father left the room without offering to make him a cup of tea too. He had never liked Zack, but even so...

'What are you doing here, Zack?' she pointedly repeated her initial question to him.

He gave a grimace. 'Besides upsetting your father, you mean?'

'Yes,' she acknowledged drily. 'Besides that.'

He shrugged, still wearing the denims and cream shirt he had worn earlier. 'I telephoned about half an hour ago to tell you I've spoken to Greg and Emily again, and they have agreed to sit down and discuss their engagement with us tomorrow evening. Tonight is out of the question, for obvious reasons,' he dismissed. 'But I thought you would at least like to know I had made more progress in that direction. I suggested we have dinner at the house. It will be more private there, and we——'

'Zack,' she cut in patiently, 'that still doesn't tell me what you're doing *here*.'

'Ah.' He gave a self-derisive grimace. 'So it doesn't. Well, when I rang, your father said you had been sick, and——'

'And I repeat what he said: that hasn't been enough reason for you to rush to my bedside during the last two years!' she taunted, eyeing him mockingly.

'No. Well.' He looked uncomfortable, ill-at-ease.

Zack looked uncomfortable? It was so unlike him, so totally out of character... 'Zack?' she prompted suspiciously.

He was looking at her closely. 'How do you feel now?'

'Zack!' Helen wasn't about to be deviated from their original conversation, no matter how much Zack might wish she would be!

He sighed defeatedly. 'Just how incapacitated are you?'

'Why?' She still eyed him suspiciously.

'Because I'm wondering if I'll be quick enough to reach the bedroom door before you do,' he grimaced.

'Zack, you aren't making the least bit of sense.' She was becoming impatient with his evasions now. 'Why would I *want* to reach the bedroom door before you do?' She had no wish to even attempt to get out of the bed!

'So that you can stop me trying to escape out of it,' he explained mildly.

Helen's suspicion deepened. 'And why would I want to do *that*?'

'Because——' he drew in a deep breath '—you are likely to feel extremely violent towards me when I tell you that last night, when we got back to my home——'

'I've already guessed what happened next, Zack,' she cut in tautly, her cheeks burning.

He looked at her searchingly, finally shaking his head. 'Have you felt the back of your head today?'

'Felt the back——? I don't feel well enough for riddles, Zack,' she sighed wearily. She didn't even know what he was talking about any more!

He nodded. 'If you had, you would have felt the lump there. Right-hand side of your head,' he added as she gingerly probed her scalp, wincing as she touched a tender spot. 'That's right.' He pursed his lips. 'You did it last night when you fell into the hallway. There's a table there, you hit your head on it. You were unconscious for several seconds. I was checking for concussion just now,' he added softly.

Helen took all of this in slowly. Very slowly.

If she had hit her head, been unconscious for a brief time, did that mean . . . ?

She looked up at Zack with accusing eyes.

CHAPTER SEVEN

ZACK had known exactly what Helen had believed happened between them last night, couldn't help but be aware of it. And he had let her go on believing it. Why? Was it his cruel, slightly warped sense of humour at work—or something else?

For all that he had joked minutes ago about her becoming violent once she knew the truth about last night, he didn't seem in any hurry to get away now, shrugging dismissively. 'When I rang and your father said you had been sick since you got in I thought I had better check that it wasn't because of any after-effects from last night——'

'Oh, it is after-effects from last night,' she nodded grimly, anger starting to build up inside her. How dared he? How *dared* he? 'I've eaten—or drunk—something that has disagreed with me!'

Zack nodded thoughtfully. 'I believe you could be right. Your pupil reaction was——'

'Damn my pupil reaction!' she cut in forcefully, grey eyes blazing accusingly.

Zack eyed her thoughtfully. 'Is this my cue to make a run for the door?'

'It's your cue to leave the house altogether!' Helen glowered up at him, throwing back the bedclothes to attempt to struggle out of bed, the cotton nightshirt she wore more than adequate covering. Even if it weren't, she wasn't sure that she would particularly care at that moment! 'You deliberately let me believe—knew that I thought—that I imagined——'

'Helen,' he cut in quietly. 'I did share my bed with you last night,' he told her with gentle apology for bursting her bubble of indignant anger.

And he did burst it, with just those few words, and Helen sank back down on to the bed. For a few minutes she had dared to hope, to believe. It was true after all, then; she really didn't remember Zack making love to her the night before.

Zack was watching her closely, his gaze intent. 'Is that really so awful?' he prompted softly. And then when she didn't—couldn't respond, 'It won't affect the divorce, you know,' he rasped disgustedly at her reaction. 'We haven't got to start all over again; one night in the same bed doesn't constitute a reconciliation.'

She didn't care about the divorce any more, nor about the extra wait because of Zack's lack of agreement to September. It really didn't seem to matter any more, when she loved this man more than life itself.

But she still had her pride where he was concerned. It was all she had left, and she clung to it like a drowning man.

'In that case,' she said briskly, 'it might be best if we both try to forget it ever happened.'

'*Can* you forget it?' His voice was a husky caress.

She couldn't *remember*, that was the trouble. But the time they had made love two years ago was forever etched into her memory.

'Can you, Helen?' Zack pushed at her lack of reply, his expression tense.

For a moment, a wild, reckless moment, she felt herself mesmerised by those dark, compelling eyes, wanted to tell him how she had never forgotten the first time they made love, that she would wake up in her bed at night sometimes hot and feverish, her dreams of their time together vivid, emotional dreams that left her feeling weak, and strangely unable to go back to sleep. But she couldn't tell Zack about those dreams, could never tell anyone about them, tried to pretend even to herself that they didn't really happen.

Her head went back defensively. 'Can you?' she challenged in return. 'And will you tell——?' She broke off abruptly, closing her eyes briefly as she realised that she had been about to act like that shrew her father had accused her of being earlier. Olivia had a husband as Zack had a wife, and, although Olivia's husband was in a wheelchair, that didn't mean that they didn't have a physical relationship in their marriage. *She* was Zack's wife; why should he tell the other woman they had gone to bed together last night? But nevertheless Helen couldn't help wondering if he would, and what he would actually say,

'Will I tell...?' Zack prompted softly at her sudden silence.

She shook her head. 'It wasn't important.' She couldn't, mustn't allow her life to be destroyed a second time by thoughts of Zack with his mistress. Because she knew that, if she hadn't found out about Olivia, she might have tried to hang on to her marriage two years ago.

Zack still frowned. 'Helen, do you——?' He turned impatiently towards the door as it swung open and Helen's father walked in un-announced with the cup of tea he had prom-ised her.

He looked from Helen's flushed face to Zack's cold annoyance. 'Has the doctor sat-isfied himself as to the patient's condition?' he taunted, his gaze challengingly on the other man as he handed Helen the tea.

Her hands were shaking so much that she had to clasp the saucer with both of them to stop the cup from rattling precariously in it; as it was she spilt some of the tea out of the cup before she had a chance to put the saucer down on the bedside table.

'I've always been satisfied with Helen's condition,' Zack told the other man goad-ingly.

A ruddy hue darkened her father's cheeks at the innuendo, and Helen turned to give Zack an impatient glare for being so deliberately provocative. 'Well, at the moment, the ''patient'' would like the privacy of her bedroom back,' she told them both pointedly. 'It's become like Spaghetti Junction in here the last half an hour,' she grumbled. 'So much for the sick-bed! If the two of you wouldn't mind, I would like to go and have a leisurely bath before getting ready for the party tonight——'

'You aren't going to the party,' Zack cut in arrogantly.

She turned to look at him slowly. 'I most certainly am,' she told him firmly, her brows raised pointedly.

His mouth firmed angrily. 'You're ill,' he reminded her hardly.

'I'm well aware of how I feel, Zack,' she bit out irritably, certainly not about to admit to him just how awful she felt. She *had* to go to Emily's party tonight—even more so if her father intended going; God knew what would happen if she wasn't there to get between the two men if they should start arguing. 'And I am going to the party tonight,' she added with finality.

Zack glared at her frustratedly, so obviously fighting a battle within himself, instinctively wanting to order her into bed with instructions not to move out of there again until he had decided she was well enough to do so, but at the same time knowing that he didn't have the right to tell her to do anything any more. And, from the stubborn expression on Helen's face, she wasn't about to give him that right either!

She certainly wasn't! All she wanted was a couple of hours' peace and quiet to prepare herself, mentally as well as physically, for the ordeal of the evening ahead. And she already knew that it was going to be that; it could hardly be anything else, with the newly engaged couple, her father, Zack and herself all present in the same room!

'I'll show you out, Neilson,' her father told him stiltedly, holding the bedroom door open for him pointedly.

Helen shot Zack an apologetic look for being the one to give her father the ammunition with which to hit out yet again at the other man.

She should have known, from her own experiences with him, that Zack wouldn't be hit!

He strolled across the bedroom to stand beside her, clasping her arms firmly in his hands to pull her to her feet in front of him, dark eyes dancing with mocking humour before he bent his head and kissed her lingeringly on the lips. She heard her father's gasp, but she was too stunned by Zack's actions to resist—in fact she responded. Instinctively, she tried to reassure herself, knowing all the time that she probably would have reacted in exactly the same way even if she hadn't been taken completely by surprise!

Her cheeks were red, her eyes feverishly bright, her lips full from the pressure of his by the time he released her a few minutes later. Dark eyes gently teased the look of mortification on her flushed face.

'I'll see you at the party,' he murmured confidently. It was a threat as well as a promise!

Helen dared a glance at her father just then. Oh, God, if looks could kill! Oh, damn both of them. Why couldn't they both just have left her here to die in peace? And, despite her defiant claim to Zack about going to the party, dying was actually what she felt like doing. Her head ached—from her fall the previous evening, she now realised!—her stomach hurt, and she still felt sick.

But she would go to Emily's party now if she had to crawl there on her hands and knees!

'Stubborn female,' Zack murmured almost admiringly, as if he was able to read her defiant thoughts easily.

Helen heaved a sigh of relief when the two men finally left, together—her father seemed about to make sure that Zack was safely off the premises!—and she at last had her bedroom back to herself. What a wonderful evening this promised to be!

The music and chatter was just as noisy as she had predicted it would be when there were a hundred or so teenagers together in one room. It took her father only a few minutes to decide to retreat to a corner of the room, away from the main throng.

And Helen had been given a brief respite from Zack too; he had been called out to an emergency at the hospital at the last minute, but he had assured Greg that he would join them all as soon as he possibly could. His 'emergency' could keep him away all evening as far as Helen was concerned. It brought back all too vividly the memories of how she had questioned the validity of those calls, to herself at least, when the two of them were still living together and Barbara had told her about Olivia. Perhaps the other woman was his 'emergency' tonight, as she had guessed she might have been in the past.

And so Helen could concentrate her energies, such as they were, on ensuring that everyone who was here enjoyed themselves. They did all seem to be, when she circulated among them, a happy bunch of teenagers intent on having a good time, and, like most teenagers, when the food was put out by the hotel staff it quickly disappeared into the ever-hungry mouths.

Emily and Greg were constantly on the move from one group of friends to another, a popular couple with both sexes, their engagement obviously a subject of great excitement—among the female guests, at least. And one or two of the young women looked disappointed that Greg was no longer available to them!

Helen watched the young couple during a brief rest from playing hostess, an emotional lump in her throat as Emily turned and laughed at something Greg had said to her, green eyes glowing. Zack was right, they did look good together! Which meant it was going to be all the more difficult to try to persuade them that they should wait a while before actually getting married; the way they looked at each other, an immediate wedding might be more appropriate!

'Dance, Mrs Neilson?'

She turned sharply at the sound of that huskily teasing voice, her breath catching in her throat as she saw how handsome Zack looked in the black evening suit and snowy-white shirt. He must have cut a dashing figure at the hospital earlier—if that was really where he had been!—in this outfit. Helen, much against her instincts, more because she didn't really have anything else than a genuine desire to actually wear the dress again after last night, was wearing the blue cashmere.

'No, thank you,' she refused stiltedly. 'And the name is Palmer!'

'The name is Neilson,' he returned firmly, head tilted slightly in challenge. 'For the next few years it is, anyway,' he added grimly, his gaze critical now as it swept over her assessingly. 'You look pale,' he announced flatly.

She knew exactly how she looked, had seen her reflection in the mirror of the ladies' powder-room here not half an hour ago. And she felt even worse than she looked. But she had almost got through the evening un-scathed; another couple of hours and she could go home and quietly collapse!

The ache in her stomach had now been joined by an occasional stabbing pain that had her almost doubled over with agony. But if she concentrated very hard—which was probably the reason she looked so pale—then she managed not to actually gasp and double up when the pain hit her. It would be a long time before she went back to that particular restaurant again, even if it was Emily's fa-vourite, sure now that she had to be suffering from food poisoning of some sort; a simple hangover wouldn't continue to make her feel this ill—in fact, get worse.

'Have you been sick again since I saw you last?' Zack probed frowningly.

'Zack!' Helen reproved as one of Emily's friends walked past with a laden plate of food and obviously heard the remark, looking down at the food she carried with suspicion now. Which wasn't fair to the hotel; they had provided a beautiful buffet supper.

'Well—have you?' Zack wasn't about to be diverted.

She had. Twice. Both times when the pain was at its worst. 'No.' She steadily met his gaze with her own.

His mouth thinned with disapproval. 'Little liar!'

Her cheeks flushed with colour at his accuracy. 'You——'

He shook his head. 'I would love to get you up on an examination table—— Don't even try and be funny,' he warned at her mocking expression. 'This isn't a laughing matter.'

Helen gave a wan smile. 'You would rather I cried?'

'If that's what you feel like doing, yes!' he rasped. 'You're too damned controlled all the time, Helen.'

'*I'm* too controlled?' she repeated incredulously. 'There speaks the eternal ice-man!'

He shook his head. 'Not with you, Helen,' he said gruffly. 'Never any more with you.'

She looked at him searchingly, puzzled by this different—even more unfathomable!— Zack. 'I don't——'

'Zack, you finally made it!' An exuberant Emily, high on being the centre of attention at her party, and also a little on the wine Helen had been monitoring her drinking, called across the room as she spotted him talking to her mother. 'I'm so glad you did.'

He shot Helen a rueful grimace. 'Much as I love our daughter, her timing needs a little working on!' he muttered before turning to open his arms to Emily as she launched herself at him as if she hadn't seen him for weeks rather than the hours it really was. 'Careful,' he warned indulgently as she almost knocked him off-balance in her enthusiasm. 'Remember the rapidly advancing years!'

Our daughter... The two words kept resounding in Helen's head. If only Emily had been their daughter. But then Emily couldn't have fallen in love with Greg, want to marry him, look so incredibly happy at being able to do so. Helen gave a rueful smile as another thought occurred to her.

'I'll be there in a moment, Emily,' Zack told her distractedly when she tried to drag him across the room to be introduced to some of her friends, his gaze fixed questioningly on Helen. 'What is it?' he prompted once he had persuaded Emily to rejoin Greg.

Helen shook her head. 'I was just thinking how you had got your way after all; when Emily marries Greg she *will* always be your daughter!' Ironically, he had got his own way once again.

'I meant *stepdaughter*, Helen,' he grated. 'Whether Emily and Greg ever get married will make no difference—— What is it?' He frowned his concern as a pain suddenly hit her without warning and she was unable to stop the involuntary gasp, a hand at her side where the pain felt worst. 'How long have you been like this?' He clasped her arm to guide her away from the party towards the door. 'And I want the truth this time, Helen,' he prompted in a voice that brooked no evasion this time.

If she was honest, and with herself she could be, then she had been feeling decidedly off-colour all week. But she hadn't really had the time to think about it, had been too busy working and making sure all the last-minute plans for this party went smoothly.

'A while, hm?' Zack said astutely, eyes narrowed in thought. 'I can't be sure, of course, not without giving you a thorough examination——'

'Which you most certainly aren't going to do!' Helen put in firmly, the pain and nausea fading again now. Until the next time. 'I have my own doctor who can do that, if necessary, thank you,' she added primly.

Zack was shaking his head even as she spoke. 'He isn't going to get the chance to examine you either. I'm taking you straight to the hospital,' he added as she would have protested.

'Hospital?' This time she didn't allow her protest to be talked down. 'Don't be so ridiculous! There's no——'

'Helen, I think the after-effects from last night may actually be masking what's really wrong with you,' he cut in with quiet authority. 'I can't be a hundred per cent sure, of course, but I think you could have appendicitis.'

Helen looked at him blankly. He couldn't be serious.

'We'll just have to hope that it's nothing worse than that,' he added grimly.

Worse? Appendicitis—if it really was that—would be bad enough, would incapacitate her for weeks. Would totally disrupt her private and business life.

She couldn't have appendicitis!

'Appendicitis,' Zack's female colleague at the hospital confirmed a short time later after a brief examination. 'All the classic signs of acute appendicitis.'

It wasn't in the least reassuring to be told her symptoms were the 'classic' ones for that particular affliction!

She had avoided even looking at Zack during the gentle but thorough examination she was subjected to, fought against showing just how much discomfort she was in, although she knew the pain must have shown on her face.

By the time they reached the hospital the pain had been so bad, she was only vaguely aware of the way the staff in the emergency department had jumped to attention once Zack had been recognised and they realised they had their senior consultant surgeon in their midst. Helen had found the strength to protest slightly when he had given her name as Helen Neilson, and himself as her closest relative. But she might as well have saved herself the energy; once again Zack was determined to have his own way.

He had refused to let her walk into the hospital, insisting on carrying her through to an examination-room, sending for his assistant, Dr Mason, to come and examine her, the surgeon turning out to be a beautiful woman in her late thirties; trust Zack to surround himself with beautiful women!

But the other woman was pleasant enough, her examination gentle, her manner warm and friendly. 'Who's going to operate, Zack?' She turned to look at him enquiringly.

Zack still looked down at Helen, her face chalk-white now, the gentle but firm proddings of his assistant having caused her more pain. 'I want you to do it,' he told the other woman without even turning his attention away from Helen. 'I'll observe, of course,' he added arrogantly.

'Of course.' Dr Mason nodded abruptly, standing up. 'I'll go and check on Theatre.'

'Er—excuse me.' Helen spoke up firmly as the other woman would have left the room. 'This is my body the two of you are talking about cutting open,' she bit out tautly. 'No one asked me if I even want this operation, let alone who is going to do it!'

'It isn't really a question of whether you want the operation, Helen,' Zack rasped, dark eyes compelling. 'Acute appendicitis means that it's an emergency. We either operate or the appendix bursts. And then you're really in trouble.'

She knew that, damn it, she wasn't stupid! She just slightly resented being talked about by these two in this briskly professional way, as if she were some inanimate object in need of repair. 'What I'm trying to tell you, Doctor, is that your bedside manner leaves a lot to be desired!' she snapped.

She knew that particular rebuke had been a mistake even as she uttered it, could see by the way Zack's eyes began to gleam with wicked humour that he thought so too, a mocking smile beginning to curve his lips. Helen glanced uncomfortably towards the woman who still stood in the doorway, watching the two of them curiously. The remark had been meant for Dr Mason as much as for Zack, and yet as Helen turned back to him she knew he was going to take it on a much more personal level!

'That isn't what you said last night,' he told her with seductive softness.

She gave a low groan even as the colour stained her cheeks, hardly daring to look at Dr Mason now. The other woman appeared not to have a sense of humour, or perhaps she just thought that Zack should be taking all of this more seriously; whatever the reason, she simply watched them, still with raised brows.

Zack sobered at the sound of Helen's embarrassment, turning to his colleague. 'As soon as possible,' he instructed curtly.

Helen was vaguely aware of the other woman leaving as she looked up at Zack with apprehensive eyes now. 'I'm frightened, Zack,' she admitted softly as he looked at her enquiringly, tightly gripping his hand as he held it out to her.

His gaze softened. 'You look as young as Emily at this moment!' He gave a rueful shake of his head. 'You——'

'Oh, God, Zack, I completely forgot, my father is still sitting outside in the waiting-room,' she remembered with dismay at this reminder of her family, thoughts of Emily naturally leading on to ones of her father. He had insisted on coming to the hospital with them once he had discovered that was where Zack was taking her. Emily had wanted to come too once she'd found out, but Zack had at least persuaded *her* that they couldn't *all* leave the party, that he would call her as soon as she knew anything. Helen's father hadn't been so easily put off, his displeasure at being anywhere near Zack a tangible thing as he sat in the back of Zack's car on the drive to the hospital. 'You'll have to go and tell him——'

'I'll go out and talk to your father in a few minutes,' Zack soothed firmly. 'At this moment I'm more concerned about you.'

'But——'

'No buts, Helen,' he told her sternly. 'It's time you started thinking of yourself rather than the needs of other people all the time. Your father is an adult, so is Emily; let them worry over you a little for a change,' he ordered cajolingly. 'You, young lady, are going to be just fine, if you'll only stop worrying about everyone else's feelings!'

She swallowed hard; she had never been in hospital for any reason other than giving birth to Emily, and was more than a little nervous about being here at all. Which, considering she had been married to a senior consultant, was a little silly. But she couldn't help the way she felt!

'Stay with me, Zack.' Her fingers tightened about his hand. 'I—I need you.' It was the first time she could ever remember saying those words. To anyone. And she had said them to Zack...

His eyes darkened, and he looked as if he would like to make some response to that remark, and then he simply nodded his head, bending down to gently brush her lips with his.

Helen reached up and put her arms about his neck, drawing him down to her, deepening the kiss, putting all her strained emotions into it.

Zack's lips moved searchingly against hers, his mood changing suddenly as the kiss became almost savage in its intensity, his hands moving against her restlessly. And then he seemed to realise where they were, why they were here, his lips no longer demanding but gently reassuring again as he gave her light butterfly kisses. 'I'll stay with you,' he assured her gruffly.

Helen would have liked to say more, but there was no more time for further conversation as, after the briefest of knocks, Dr Mason came back into the room to say that Theatre were ready for them now.

The nursing staff instantly set about preparing Helen for surgery, although Zack kept his word and stayed in the room with her, in softly spoken consultation with Dr Mason while this was going on. It was amazing how reassured Helen felt just having him in the same room with her.

He did leave her briefly at her urging, to go and reassure her father, and to talk to Emily on the telephone, but he was back in time to accompany her down to the operating theatre.

'All right, Helen?' Dr Mason smiled down at her reassuringly, wearing her theatre greens now.

Zack's face was the last thing Helen saw before the blackness of the anaesthetic claimed her...

And it was the first thing she saw when she woke up again!

It was pitch black outside the window across from the bed, only a small lamp shining above the bed behind her, an eerie silence

outside in the corridor to confirm that it was
still night-time.

The nagging ache of a pain, accompanied
by the occasional stabbing ones, had gone
now, her side curiously numb instead at the
moment, although she had no doubt she
would feel it again later, once the anaesthetic
had worn off completely! There was a bandage strapped about her wrist to keep a splint
attached to her arm, and she knew that beneath that bandage she had a needle in her
hand, where she was being fed glucose intra-
venously from the bag suspended on the pole
beside the bed. At the moment this felt more
uncomfortable and restricting than her side!

And Zack sat in the bedside chair, his head
slumped down on to his chest in sleep, a
strangely vulnerable-looking Zack she felt almost maternal concern for. He must have
been here hours!

He had discarded the jacket to his dinner
suit some time during the night and hung it on
the back of his chair, the bow-tie was gone
too, the top button of his shirt undone. His
arms were folded across his chest, his hair
lightly ruffled, as if recently mussed by the
length of his fingers running through it. He

looked younger with his hair ruffled like that, his face softened in sleep, all hardness erased, the fierceness of that dark gaze covered by heavy lids, his lashes long and thick against his cheeks.

As Helen gazed her fill of him she realised that it was the first time she had ever seen him asleep . . .

It was a strange admission to have to make about her own husband. It wasn't as if they had never made love, they had just never 'slept together'!

At least, not that she remembered.

She closed her eyes almost guiltily at the intimacy of her thoughts, but not before she had seen Dr Mason enter the room. It had been an instinctive reaction as soon as she heard the turning of the door-handle, feeling foolish at being found lying here gazing at her own husband, desperately trying to remember still being with him the previous evening. Thank God Zack hadn't woken up and seen her; she was sure that her expression would have betrayed her love for him.

But she heard him stir in the chair now as he sensed the other woman's presence in the room, could only lie here and imagine the sleepy sensuality of those dark eyes, the warm, uncomplicated smile he would bestow on his assistant.

'Has she woken yet?' Dr Mason asked softly.

'Just a few mutterings in her sleep,' Zack dismissed, yawning tiredly. 'I'm afraid I fell asleep myself.'

'Why don't you get off home?' Dr Mason prompted concernedly. 'I'll have someone call you as soon as she wakes up.'

'No, I promised Helen I would stay with her,' he stated with finality.

Helen felt like a complete fraud now; she knew that Zack needed his sleep, and that there was no reason why he shouldn't go home and have some! The thing was, how could she arrange to wake up in a way that would look totally convincing? How did one wake up?

Before she could devise any plans for doing that Zack spoke again. 'Why don't you go home?' he suggested softly to the other woman. 'I can do whatever needs to be done here. There's no point in both of us having a sleepless night,' he reasoned.

'Are you sure?' The other woman hesitated.

'Very,' Zack dismissed lightly. 'Oh, and Olivia—thanks,' he added warmly, the door clicking seconds later as the other woman left the room.

Olivia? Helen heard the name in disbelief. Dr Mason, Zack's colleague, was *Olivia*, the woman he had been in love with for years?

CHAPTER EIGHT

HELEN looked at the other woman with new, enlightened eyes, when she came in to check on her the next morning.

She had lain in stunned silence for a long time after Olivia Mason had left her room the night before, had been completely oblivious to Zack's restless movements about the room, as she reassessed all her preconceived ideas about the 'other woman' in her marriage!

For some reason she had imagined Olivia to be a small, clinging blonde—she didn't know why she had thought that, but she had!—a pathetic victim of circumstances that kept her tied to her crippled husband, someone Zack had possibly met because of her husband's accident. Instead, Olivia Mason was a tall, more-than-capable brunette, very beautiful, was a colleague of Zack's. Somehow Helen thought she preferred her preconceived ideas about the other woman rather than the reality!

Helen had finally 'appeared' to wake up the previous night, reassuring Zack that she felt very well after the operation—the shock she had just received was another matter entirely!—insisting he go home and get some rest. She was deliberately brusque with him, remembering, to her consternation, how she had pleaded with him to stay with her before she went for her operation last night, told him she needed him. She was mortified, in the light of who Dr Mason had turned out to be, at her own weakness. She certainly had no intention of clinging to him again, cutting through Zack's protests by pointing out that it was the sensible thing to do. His gaze was searching on the paleness of her face before he finally agreed to leave, accepting the sense of being rested for the following day.

Helen's first visitor of the day was Olivia Mason, come to check on her patient!

In the light of what Helen now knew about the other woman and Zack, she couldn't help wondering if the other woman's visit was completely professional. And then she chided herself for being so ridiculous; as colleagues at the hospital, Zack and Olivia had plenty of opportunity to meet and be together, without the other woman being reduced to visiting Helen in the real hope that Zack would be there.

Then curiosity, perhaps, about the woman she knew Zack had married so calculatedly, now that Helen wasn't doubled up with pain? That, surely, would be perfectly natural in the circumstances? Helen knew that *she* was curious about the other woman, so why shouldn't Olivia feel the same way about her?

Olivia Mason was all professional efficiency this morning as she dealt with the examination smoothly. 'As long as there are no complications—and I don't see any reason that there should be—we should be able to allow you to go home by the end of the week,' she announced as she straightened the bedclothes.

'How soon will I be able to get back to work?' Helen voiced her anxiety.

'As soon as *I* say you can,' cut in a deep, authoritative voice before Olivia Mason could make a reply.

Helen looked past the woman to find Zack standing in the doorway. 'I was only——'

'I know exactly what you "were only",' he acknowledged grimly, walking purposefully across the room to stand beside the bed. 'You aren't going back to work until you're completely well again. I spoke to Sonia earlier this morning, and she assures me she can manage perfectly well——'

'You had no right!' Helen bristled indignantly, attempting to sit up, and then falling back again with a pained groan as she found that the movement pulled on her wound.

'I have every right,' he returned with his usual arrogance, her discomfort seeming to prove his point. 'You seem to forget, I own the damned shop!'

Angry colour darkened her cheeks. 'I might have known you would throw that up at me!' she flared. 'You only own the building still, I bought the business,' she reminded him defiantly.

'And you need that building to be able to run that business,' he pointed out softly.

Her eyes widened at the veiled threat. 'Why, you rotten——'

'I think it's time I left,' Olivia Mason put in firmly, her smile rueful as she looked at Zack. 'Lunch?'

'Fine.' He nodded terse agreement to the suggestion, but his attention was still grimly fixed on Helen as the other woman left the room.

Helen's anger turned to despair. In front of her, right here in front of her, the two of them had arranged to meet for lunch. She knew she didn't have a marriage with Zack, that they were getting a divorce, that the other woman must know all of that, and yet there was something humiliating still about Zack arranging to meet his mistress in front of his wife!

'Helen, you——' Zack broke off as he noticed the tears falling silently down her cheeks. 'Oh, hell!' he swore softly to himself before moving to gather her up in his arms. 'Here I am, the experienced doctor, and I'm shouting and bullying you only hours after you've had a general anaesthetic.' His voice was full of self-disgust. 'I didn't mean it, Helen; I was only, in my usual heavy-handed way, trying to show you how strongly I feel about your being completely well before you even attempt to go back to work.'

She couldn't seem to stop crying once she had started, deep, racking sobs that really bore absolutely no relation to what had just taken place. Zack had tried to bully her—that was certainly nothing new!—Zack had arranged to have lunch with the woman he loved—he was perfectly entitled to do that!—so she didn't know why she was this upset.

'You're going to drown the both of us if you don't stop soon!' Zack finally teased lightly.

She gave a choked laugh now. 'I'm sorry.' She hiccuped inelegantly as she moved slightly away from him. 'I don't know what happened.' She shook her head, wiping the tears from her cheeks with her fingers, feeling exhausted now by the show of emotion.

'People are often over-emotional after a general anaesthetic,' Zack dismissed. 'It's a natural reaction.'

She eyed him derisively, resting back against the pillows now. 'I don't suppose your arrogance had anything to do with it?'

He relaxed slightly, his mouth twisting wryly. 'I'll admit I could have been a little more tactful in my approach—all right, a *lot* more,' he accepted drily at her scathing look. 'But Sonia *can* manage until——'

'That's it, add insult to injury by telling me I'm completely superfluous!' Helen shook her head in rueful disbelief at his complete lack of sensitivity.

His gaze darkened on the shapeliness of her breasts beneath the cotton gown she wore. 'I didn't say that,' he murmured provocatively.

Her cheeks felt warm at this introduction of intimacy between them, but she met his gaze unflinchingly—to her credit! 'Is that why my family is beating a path to my door?' She deliberately misunderstood him, all too aware that, whatever game he was playing with her, it was Olivia Mason he was taking out to lunch later.

'I knew there was something I meant to ask you when I came in!' he said with mock horror at his oversight. 'Do you feel up to visitors? Emily has been chafing to get here since eight o'clock this morning, and Greg is anxious to see you too. They both stayed at the house last night, I discovered when I got up this morning,' he explained dismissively.

Emily in the bedroom she had kept for herself there...

'They're both outside in the waiting-room,' Zack added encouragingly.

Helen couldn't help noticing that any interest in her welfare on her father's part, despite his insistence in coming to the hospital the night before, seemed to be lacking this morning.

Zack frowned as he saw the shadow that briefly crossed her face. 'Since I went out to the waiting-room last night to tell him what was happening, I haven't seen or heard from your father, Helen,' he told her gently. 'He got a taxi home as far as I know,' he shrugged.

It was amazing how Zack had so easily guessed the reason for her sudden dismay. 'I'll see if I can telephone him later——'

'Helen, you're the patient, let him be the one to come to you,' Zack cut in exasperatedly. 'I strongly advise against putting yourself under pressure in this way. Just forget about the lot of them; they are all more than capable of looking after themselves. And that isn't said to make you feel superfluous,' he added quickly. 'I just don't think you should be giving yourself any worries just now.'

That was easier said than done, although Emily's cheerful face did a lot to make her feel better when Zack brought the young couple into the room a few minutes later, Greg at Emily's side. *That* was something Helen knew she would have to get used to!

'You missed a great party, Mummy!' Emily grinned down at her after kissing her warmly on the cheek and presenting her with a bunch of carnations.

Helen raised her eyes heavenwards. '"How awful for you, Mummy,"' she mimicked. '"I'm so glad it's all over and you're starting to get better,"' she added drily, at the same time returning her daughter's smile as the latter sat on the side of the bed.

'It must be something in the delivery!' Zack said wryly, shaking his head. 'I assured your mother the shop, and you, can manage perfectly well without her, and she almost ripped me to verbal shreds for my trouble,' he explained to Emily and Greg as they looked at him enquiringly. 'You more or less tell her she isn't even missed and end up getting hugged for it!' He sighed heavily, as if the workings of the female mind were just too complex for him!

Which Helen knew perfectly well they weren't! Zack knew exactly what he was doing where women were concerned. Olivia

Mason appeared to be the only one he hadn't completely succeeded with, and that had only been because of the unfavourable circumstances in which their love had blossomed. A shadow darkened Helen's face at the thought of the two of them together.

Greg grinned across at his father. 'It's in the delivery,' he confirmed with a mocking inclination of his head.

Zack shook his head again. 'There's no justice in the world!'

Emily eyed him speculatively. 'Does that mean you would have liked a hug too?'

Helen's cheeks blazed with colour at the sudden intimate turn the conversation had taken, inwardly berating herself for blushing so easily as Zack turned to look at her searchingly. No doubt *Olivia* wouldn't behave so gauchely!

'I think we're embarrassing your mother,' Zack finally said drily. 'And you, Emily, are going to get the sharp edge of Sister's tongue if she sees you sitting on the side of the bed,' he warned derisively. 'It isn't allowed.'

Emily grinned at the silliness of such a rule, but she stood up anyway.

Helen only half listened to the light-hearted exchange, although she was grateful for the change of subject. But she was starting to feel very tired now, was amazed at how weak she felt from just a few minutes' conversation. She looked up to find Zack still watching her intently.

'Right, you two.' He spoke briskly to the young couple. 'You've reassured yourselves that I didn't whisk Helen away last night for any nefarious purposes of my own, that she is, in fact, fine; now I think it's time we all left and let her get some sleep.'

'But——'

'We——'

'I could make it "doctor's orders" if you would like,' he added mildly, but there was a steel edge to his voice none the less.

'You aren't my doctor, Dr Mason is,' Helen put in softly, slightly challenging, despite the fact that he was right about her needing to get some sleep.

'I—what the hell——?' Zack turned towards the door with a frown as there was the sound of raised voices out in the corridor, his mouth tightening as he crossed the room to look outside, only to be pushed aside seconds later when Helen's father strode purposefully into the room. So much for his heart condition now, Helen thought ruefully, as he was determined that his way wouldn't be barred by the younger man.

'I'm sorry, Mr Neilson.' A flustered-looking nurse followed closely behind him, her youthful face flushed with indignation. 'I tried to tell this gentleman——'

'I am not "this gentleman"!' Helen's father snapped angrily. 'I am Mrs *Neilson's* father!'

The young nurse ignored the tirade, still looking apologetically at Zack.

He smiled back at her reassuringly. 'It's all right, Nurse,' he soothed gently. 'We will all be leaving in a few minutes, so that Mrs Neilson can get some much-needed rest.'

'Mrs *Neilson*,' Helen's father echoed disgustedly as the young nurse thankfully left the room. 'I came here to see Helen, and I'm told they don't have a Mrs *Palmer* here at all, but that Mr Neilson is visiting his *wife*. Even once I've established that this is Helen, I'm still told I can't even come in to see my own daughter——'

'There's a reason for that, Edward——'

Pale blue eyes blazed his dislike for the younger man. 'I'm sure *you've* always got a ready explanation for everything!'

Zack's mouth tightened at the insult, a nerve pulsing in his jaw, and Helen, at least, recognised the danger signals. 'Dad——'

'The—reason—for—that, Edward,' Zack bit out with careful control, 'is that only two visitors are allowed in at any one time, especially when Helen so recently had her operation, and Emily and Greg——'

'And you,' her father put in accusingly. 'Even I can add that up to three!'

Zack's teeth clamped together. 'I'm a doctor,' he grated.

'And I'm Helen's father!'

'You're certainly no gentleman,' Zack rasped with distaste.

'Why, you arrogant young——'

'Stop it, Gramps!' Emily cut in tautly as her grandfather took a threatening step towards Zack. 'Just stop it!' Bright angry colour blazed in her cheeks. 'Mummy hasn't been well. She certainly doesn't need you coming here, throwing your weight about like a spoilt child——'

'Emily...!' Helen gasped weakly.

'How dare you?' Her father completely ignored her, his indignation all turned on Emily now.

And Helen wondered how Emily 'dared' either, staring at her daughter—as she stood with her body rigid, her hands clenched into fists at her sides—in mute horror and fascination; apart from Zack no one had ever stood up to her father in this way. She had certainly never seen Emily show such temper before where her grandfather was concerned.

'How dare you?' Helen's father repeated with incredulous fury. 'My God.' He turned disgustedly on Zack. 'A few weeks in your son's company and Emily has become as rude and rebellious as he is——'

'Now listen here,' Greg cut in indignantly.

'Greg isn't rude and rebellious,' Emily defended heatedly, almost stamping her foot in her anger.

'He's his father's son——'

'Thank God for that,' Emily snapped coldly, very beautiful in her defensive fury. 'Zack and Greg are both wonderful——'

'Unlike me, I suppose?' her grandfather scorned.

Helen wanted to intervene, to stop this now, but the two opponents were so intent on each other at this moment that she didn't think they would even hear anyone else. She just couldn't believe this was actually happening!

Emily's eyes flashed like emeralds. 'You said it,' she answered her grandfather. 'I didn't!'

He looked at her coldly. 'I didn't come here to be insulted——'

'Then why did you come here?' Emily challenged, her hands still clenching and unclenching at her sides. 'You haven't even said hello to Mummy yet, let alone asked her how she is——'

'I can see how she is!' He looked down at Helen disgustedly. 'You were a fool ever to marry Neilson,' he rasped with open dislike. 'And you'll be even more of a fool if you allow Emily to marry his son!'

Helen was totally speechless, still staring at her furious daughter; she had *never* seen Emily like this.

'Mummy isn't the fool—you are,' Emily told her grandfather heavily, some of her anger seeming to deflate as she looked at him pityingly. 'You don't like to see people happy, you always want to ruin everything.'

'I refuse to stay here and listen to any more of this,' her grandfather told her with stiff dignity, standing very tall and erect, turning cold eyes on Helen as she lay pale in the bed. 'I will talk to you again, Helen, when I know you have come to your senses and forbidden this engagement.' And with one last glare of intense dislike in Zack's direction he turned and left the room as abruptly as he had entered it minutes earlier.

Helen swallowed hard, slumping back weakly against the pillows; if she had felt exhausted before she now felt totally shattered!

She had never seen Emily this upset. Her daughter had been a placid baby, a happy little girl, only mildly rebellious as a young teenager, and the only time Helen could remember Emily being stubbornly angry had been when she had been told the marriage to Zack was at an end and they were moving out into their own house. Even then Emily's anger had been of a silent, reproachful kind, and as there had really been nothing Helen could do about it anyway she had just had to let time be the healer. The fact that it hadn't, that Emily had continued to spend time with her new 'family', was something Helen had learnt of only recently, yesterday, in fact!

Emily as a fierce virago was also something new to her, making her wonder just how well she knew her daughter after all!

'Drink this,' Zack encouraged gently, holding out a glass of water to her.

'Oh, Mummy, I'm so sorry!' Emily groaned her self-reproach as she saw how pale Helen had become. 'I didn't mean—it was only—I'm really sorry!' she choked before fleeing the room.

'I'll go after her,' Greg told them softly before hurrying after Emily.

Helen briefly closed her eyes, wondering if this could be part of some nightmare, the same nightmare that brought her into hospital at all. But no, when she opened her eyes again Zack was still sitting concernedly on the side of the bed, holding the glass of water she hadn't taken from him.

' "You'll feel the sharp edge of Sister's tongue if she sees you sitting on the bed like that," ' she reminded him dully, and then shook her head in self-disgust as Zack looked at her with raised brows. 'No, perhaps *you* wouldn't,' she realised with a sigh.

'I doubt it,' he acknowledged drily.

'Zack, what happened just now?' she frowned a little dazedly. 'One minute everything was light and teasing, and the next——!' She shook her head incomprehensibly.

'The next your father arrived,' Zack pointed out gently.

Her frown deepened. 'But what difference did that make?' They were all used to her father's stubbornly narrow-minded behaviour. Weren't they...?

Zack carefully put the glass of water down on the bedside table before standing up. 'Do you really want to know?' he finally said softly.

She looked up at him searchingly. 'I really want to know,' she eventually nodded, unable to read any of his thoughts from his closed expression.

He shrugged, moving restlessly about the room. 'I'm not sure this is a good idea at all,' he muttered irritably.

'I need to know, Zack,' she persuaded.

'You only had an operation last night,' he sighed. 'This situation should never have been allowed to happen at all—*I* shouldn't have allowed it to!'

Helen raised dark brows scathingly. 'Do you really think you could have stopped it?' The exchange between her father and Emily had been too heated to be interrupted, she felt.

Zack shrugged impatiently. 'I could have tried.'

'You didn't know what was going to happen.' Helen was still slightly dazed that it had!

He shook his head. 'I knew something like it was sure to happen some time in the near future, if not tonight,' he told her with a sigh.

Her eyes widened at his certainty. 'I don't see how——'

'Helen,' he cut in firmly, 'do you have any idea why Emily left home a year ago?'

She frowned, wondering why he was changing the subject. Or was he . . . ?

'Emily was going to college,' Helen said slowly, her thoughts racing. 'The flat was nearer, more convenient—— That wasn't it at all, was it?' she realised with sickening clarity.

Zack took his time about replying, obviously torn between telling her the truth, and not wanting to upset her any more today.

But in the end he gave the reply Helen had known—and dreaded!—that he would!

'Emily left home because she couldn't stand living with her grandfather any longer!'

CHAPTER NINE

'I'M REALLY sorry I had to tell you that, Helen.' Zack lightly caressed the paleness of her cheek with long, sensitive fingers. 'Especially now. But it's past time that you knew the truth.'

She hadn't realised, had never even guessed that her beloved daughter had moved out of the home they shared because of her own grandfather. Even now it was difficult to comprehend, but Zack had no reason to lie to her about it. And hadn't she seen the evidence of Emily's resentment with her own eyes . . .?

Helen looked up at Zack with pained eyes. 'But why?'

He avoided her gaze. 'Perhaps you should talk to Emily about that——'

'*You* talk to me, Zack.' Helen looked at him with pleading eyes. 'Emily has obviously confided in you.' There was no bitterness in her words, only dull acceptance of her own shortcomings; she had always believed that Emily could come to her and talk to her about anything, but the engagement to Greg, and this latest revelation about why she had left home, was proof of just how wrong she had been about that!

Zack stood up abruptly. 'She wasn't being disloyal to you——'

'I know that,' Helen sighed, knowing she had to accept, whatever her own feelings about her brief marriage to Zack, that Emily had formed a deep and lasting bond with him.

This realisation suddenly brought into stark contrast her father's relationship with Emily. He had always adhered to that old-fashioned belief, 'Children should be seen and not heard', probably because he had become a father so late in life himself, often berating Helen for being too easygoing with Emily. He had certainly never shown any interest in taking over as the father figure in Emily's life, which was probably another reason why it had been so easy for Emily to form that bond with Zack. Why had she never realised any of this before?

Zack shrugged now. 'Edward has always dominated your life, Helen; Emily was determined he wouldn't do the same to her. He has, Helen,' he insisted as she would have protested. 'The only major decision your father didn't make for you was when you married me, and *I* made that one for you,' he reminded her grimly.

God, how weak that made her sound. Helen had always believed she was an independent person, believed she made the decisions that concerned her family, whether good or bad. And maybe the small, everyday ones, she did, but Zack was right; everything else, anything major and she took a back seat while someone else made the decision. Her father had decided she had to marry Ian, even though she had known it was the wrong thing to do. When her mother had died so suddenly it was her father who had decided that they had to continue living with him. Had that been one of the reasons Ian was never home, that he'd begun to drink...? Good God, was it?

When Ian was killed her father had been the one who had told her she shouldn't work until Emily went to school, a decision that had made her totally dependent on him financially. It was a fact she had never been allowed to forget, she recalled now, her father expecting her to just take over as his housekeeper. By the time Emily was four and ready to go to school the pattern had been so well established that it was by tacit agreement that Helen had got a job which fitted in with school hours and the school holidays, her father unwilling to look after the little girl for even a few hours each day. On top of that she had still continued to cook and clean for them all—a modern-day Cinderella, no less!

But why had she never realised any of this either?

Guilt, came the immediate answer. She had let her father down, he had let her know in no uncertain terms, by becoming pregnant at only seventeen while still unmarried, and so she had spent the next eighteen years of her life trying to make restitution for the lapse!

A lot of parents would have been shocked by her pregnancy, but once that initial reaction had worn off most of them were usually supportive of whatever decision the prospective mother chose to make. But not her father. And he had never let her forget her mistake . . .

But he wasn't completely to blame for his behaviour, Helen realised; she had let him do that to her, was as much to blame for what had happened as he was. He had acted out of ignorance; she had acted out of *guilt*.

And Emily had moved out because of both of them!

'Helen——'

'It's all right, Zack.' She gave him a strained smile as she saw he was watching her anxiously. 'I'm grateful to you for showing me how weak I really——'

'That isn't what I said at all, damn it!' he rasped impatiently, eyes narrowed.

'But I have been,' she accepted with a frown, but knowing she couldn't be that way any more. She had been a coward most of her life, had almost lost her daughter because of it; now was the time to take action to stop that happening. And that was going to cause all sorts of upheaval, in the lives of others as well as her own. Her temples began to throb, and her hands clenched in tension just at the thought of it.

Zack still watched her. 'Tension is the last thing you need at the moment!'

Helen gave a wry smile. 'It's something I seem to have been avoiding most of my life.' She shook her head. Her actions all these years might have seemed like the easy way out, but when she looked back on them now she knew that she had made a lot of people, including herself, unhappy.

'Then another few days isn't going to make that much difference, is it?' Zack told her grimly. 'Your father didn't give the impression that he intends coming back at visiting time,' he rasped dismissively. 'But I'm sure Emily will be. Full of apologies for this morning, no doubt.' His mouth twisted.

Helen shook her head. 'She has nothing to apologise for.'

'This self-pity becomes you as little as playing the martyr has all these years!' Zack told her scornfully.

Her cheeks became flushed at the taunt, her eyes glittering angrily. 'You——'

'Maybe I should have stayed in your life two years ago,' he continued tauntingly. 'At least with me you retaliate!'

She drew in a sharp breath at his deliberate cruelty. 'I left you, remember?' she bit out coldly.

'Hm,' he nodded thoughtfully, seeming satisfied now that he had shaken her out of her mood of self-pity—he had been right about that, and it *was* just as unattractive as martydom! 'Maybe the two of us should sit down and discuss that some time?'

The knowledge of his relationship with the doctor who had operated on her was just too raw! 'The only thing I want to discuss with you is our divorce!'

His mouth firmed. 'I've told you——'

'I don't care what you've told me, Zack,' she snapped. 'I'm not about to waste another three years of my life married to you!'

He became suddenly still, dangerously so, the cold fury within him a tangible thing. 'What is that supposed to mean?' His voice was silkily soft. 'Did you lie about there not being a man in your life, Helen? Do you actually already have my replacement in mind; is that why you're so set on the divorce in September?'

Was she so unattractive to him that the idea of her being involved with someone else was incredible to him?

As it happened she wasn't, and she hadn't been, but up until now she had thought that was through personal choice. Now she wasn't so sure. Was it just another one of those decisions that had actually been made for her...? She didn't know any more, was starting to question all of her actions.

'Don't you have a luncheon appointment you have to go to?' she reminded Zack pointedly.

His mouth firmed. 'We were talking about you——'

'No—*you* were talking about me,' Helen corrected harshly. '*I* would like to get some rest now, I'm feeling very tired.' She knew that the reason for her complete weariness was as much due to too much emotional turmoil as to the fact that she had recently undergone an operation.

Zack seemed to realise that too, his impatient sigh full of self-recrimination. 'What the hell am I thinking of?' he muttered disgustedly. 'If someone had come in and upset one of my patients in this way I would have them barred from visiting again!'

That would be just too much to hope for, not when he was a senior consultant here!

But as far as Helen was concerned, the less she saw of him for the remainder of her stay in hospital, the better.

Especially if he intended kissing her like this each time before he left!

She had been completely unprepared for him to cross the room in long strides, bend down abruptly, and savagely claim her lips with his own. So unprepared, she responded!

Her arms moved up to encircle his neck, her fingers becoming entwined in the dark thickness of his hair, her lips parted moistly to his.

He pulled back as suddenly as he had claimed her. 'Get some rest,' he advised gruffly. 'I'll go and talk to Emily, and hopefully we can sort this mess out, once and for all.'

Not without Helen having to deal with her father, they wouldn't. But if that really was what had driven Emily away from their home then it was way past time Helen did something about it!

*   *   *

As she had been sure he wouldn't after delivering that ultimatum, her father didn't come near the hospital again while she was there. And as Helen had no intention of forbidding Emily to marry Greg she had made no effort to contact her father either; there was no point. Anyway, she needed this brief respite to think things through, mainly to decide what she was going to say to him.

Making her peace with Emily had been something she had needed to do very badly, and thankfully Emily made it very easy for her. They had talked, really talked, about the situation concerning Emily's grandfather, and, without quite knowing what was going to happen, Helen had promised her daughter that things would change once she was out of hospital. Whether her father or she should move out, she wasn't yet sure, but she knew it was time for her to be on her own at last. She felt strangely nervous about it, realised that, at thirty-five, she had never lived on her own!

By the end of the week, as predicted, Olivia Mason deemed her fit enough to go home, and with that release Helen decided that if the mountain wouldn't come to her then she would go to it! She arranged for a taxi to take her home, intending to be alone when she talked to her father, which was why she didn't let any of the family know that she had been discharged. No doubt Zack would find out soon enough and pass the information on to Emily and Greg.

Her father was sitting at the kitchen table reading the newspaper when she let herself into the house, and it was almost as if Helen were looking at him for the first time. Had he always looked this stern and unyielding, his eyes hard, deep lines of unhappiness grooved beside his nose and mouth, that mouth a thin, unsmiling line as he looked at her? Helen frowned as she tried to remember the last time she had seen him smile, let alone actually laugh out loud at something. No occasion came to mind.

'So you're back, are you?' he rasped challengingly, making no effort to stand up or see to her welfare, even though the strain on her face must have told him what an effort it had been, leaving the hospital and getting here at all.

When had he become so unyielding, so unforgiving? Or had he always been like this and she had just never noticed, accepting it be-

cause he was her father? But being geneti-
cally her father didn't give him any emotional
rights; that sort of loyalty had to be earned.
The way that Zack had in the short time he
had been Emily's stepfather... You had to
give love to be able to receive it, and Helen
now realised that her father had never done
that!

As if her brief thoughts of Zack had par-
tially transferred themselves to her father, he
looked past her into the hallway. 'Where's
Neilson?' he scorned.

Helen swayed slightly on her feet, moving
to sit on the chair opposite her father, her
movements studied, this being the longest
time she had been mobile since her operation. 'I have no idea where Zack is,' she dismissed lightly.

Her father's mouth twisted. 'Tired of you
again already, has he——?'

'I think it would be better for all of us if
you moved out of this house into a home of
your own!' She blurted out the words she had
meant to lead up to slowly during the course
of their conversation, stung into it by his
taunt. Zack had continued to visit her every
day of her stay in hospital, but he had never

kissed her again, and Helen was always left wondering if he was going off to meet Olivia Mason when those visits ended.

Her father reeled back as if she had physically struck him. 'What on earth——? Helen, have you taken leave of your senses?' He stared at her incredulously.

'No.' She gave a heavy sigh, regretting her bluntness, but perhaps, after all, it was the best way. She might have changed her mind if she had left it too long before telling him! She hoped that she wouldn't have done, but the self-doubt was still there... 'I think I've just come to them,' she told him with hard resolve. 'You have proved, while I've been in hospital, that you're more than capable of taking care of yourself.' The house was as neat and tidy as when she did the housework, and he obviously wasn't starving, looked as fit and healthy as he usually did—in fact, perhaps a little more so! 'If the time ever comes when you aren't able to do that, then we'll have to rethink the situation,' she added briskly. 'But until that time——'

'You're throwing me out!' His eyes glittered with cold accusation.

'I'm *suggesting* it might be better if you had a home of your own.' Her tone remained calm, but inside she was a churning mass of nerves, could never remember standing up to her father in this way before. My God, it was time she did!

'What about my heart condition?'

'Yes—what about that?' remarked a thoughtful voice from behind them, and Helen swung round to see Zack standing just inside the room. 'The front door was unlocked, and I heard raised voices,' he smoothly explained his intrusion.

And Helen could see by the censure in his gaze that he would want a full explanation from her in the very near future concerning her discharge from hospital this morning and the fact that she hadn't seen fit to let any of them know about it. Obviously the beautiful Olivia had told him about it, as Helen had thought she might. Helen stiffened defensively at the thought of the other woman and the place she had in Zack's life, turning away as she saw a puzzled frown replace the censure on his face when he saw her look of resentment.

'You!' Helen's father turned on him angrily. 'I should have known you were at the back of all this! You have been nothing but trouble in our life from the very beginning——'

'I'm the one who wants you to leave,' Helen cut in with quiet determination.

'Because of him,' her father accused. 'Don't you remember what it was like being married to him the last time? Have you no pride, Helen?' he added scornfully. 'Or do you still not care that he has a mistress as well as a wife?'

'You——'

'Even if he doesn't still have the same one, there are sure to be others.' Her father cut across Zack's anger. 'He's done it before. You'll never be sure, each time he's late home, that he isn't with *her* rather than working as he claims to be. You——'

'That's enough!' It was the coldly furious tone of Zack's voice that silenced the older man rather than the words themselves, brown eyes glittering dangerously. 'You're a vicious, conniving old man, Edward,' he ground out harshly. 'You could have had it all—Helen's love and loyalty—without pushing and manipulating her, using every weapon you can think of to achieve what you want for yourself rather than what's best for her, including this feeble-old-man-with-a-heart-condition act——'

'I *do* have a heart condition——'

'I'm not saying you don't. I don't think even you would go to those lengths to get your own way,' Zack dismissed disgustedly. 'Anyway, I know what condition you have, and it's perfectly stabilised by medication. There are thousands of people with the same condition who lead perfectly normal lives; there's no reason why you can't do the same. Helen is leaving with me now.' The dark blaze of his gaze silenced her as she would have protested. 'I'll arrange for you to move into a flat, Edward, where there is a warden to check on——'

'I'm not going to one of those places!' her father scoffed.

Zack shrugged. 'It's either that or an old people's home. Make your choice, Edward,' he said coldly. 'I'll call you tomorrow and you can let me know what your decision is.' He took a firm hold of Helen's arm and marched her out of the room, down the hallway, picking up her suitcase she had brought from the hospital with her on the way, and out into the sunshine.

Helen breathed deeply of the fresh, warm air. She had been dreading that confrontation with her father, and it had been every bit as awful as she had imagined it would be.

She turned to Zack with pained eyes, that last vivid picture of her father in defeat still in her mind. 'Do you think he'll be all right?' she groaned.

Zack's expression softened at her continued concern. 'I guarantee you that within a couple of months of moving in he'll be running the darned complex!'

Helen thought about that for a few moments, and realised he was probably right. Her father wouldn't be down for long. She relaxed at this reassuring knowledge.

'And now——' Zack steered her in the direction of his car where it stood parked next to the pavement ' —I think it's time the two of us did some talking of our own, don't you?'

She frowned up at him as he very firmly saw her seated in the passenger side of his car. 'What about?'

He arched dark brows. 'My mistress would be as good a place to start as any, I think . . .'

She had a sinking feeling in the pit of her stomach, had seen how angry he had become at her father's mention of the other woman. 'Olivia Mason,' she sighed resignedly.

'*More* than time the two of us talked!' Zack muttered before moving to get into the car beside her.

CHAPTER TEN

AND yet they made the drive to Zack's home in silence, and even when they got there he insisted that Helen go into the main drawing-room and lie down on the sofa, arranging for a tray of coffee to be brought in to them, before he raised the subject of Olivia again.

He sat on the edge of the sofa beside Helen, making her very aware of his closeness, his aftershave a delight to the senses. 'Who told you about Olivia?' His eyes were narrowed questioningly.

Helen shrugged. 'Your mother. She was concerned for you, Zack,' she hastened to add as his expression darkened ominously. 'Was so relieved you seemed to have got over your feelings for Olivia enough to marry me. Your mother believed our relationship was other than it was, that you would have confided your—closeness to Olivia to me. She didn't think she was doing any harm by talking to me about it,' Helen concluded lamely.

'And was she?' Zack frowned. 'I can see that she was,' he sighed as Helen felt unable to make a reply. 'Helen, I want you to know, the day of my mother's funeral there was no other woman I wanted at my side but you.' He was watching her intently as he spoke. 'Do you believe me?' he finally prompted.

She was stunned!

It couldn't be true—could it? 'But—but——'

Zack took both her hands in his own. 'Do you believe me, Helen?'

She looked up at him searchingly, at the burning intensity of his gaze, and she wanted to believe him, wanted that so much, to hope—— 'I can't.' She shook her head. 'Because whatever you say now it ultimately made no difference, did it?' She pulled her hands free of his, clasping them tightly together. 'We made love, but you still let me go when the time came.'

'You cried the day we made love,' he said gruffly.

Her eyes widened as she looked up at him dazedly. 'What?'

'I had been crying before we made love. But you cried afterwards. That was significant, don't you think?' he groaned.

Of course she had cried; it had been the most marvellous, beautiful, moving experience of her—— 'Zack...?' She frowned up at him. 'I left only because we had an arrangement, and with Barbara's death that arrangement was at an end.'

'And there was also Olivia,' he nodded.

Yes, there was Olivia. The hopes Helen had dared to give flight after Zack's earlier statement fell to the ground. 'Yes, there was Olivia,' she accepted dully.

'But that's the whole point—there *wasn't*!' he told her frustratedly. 'There hadn't been for some time, not really. Oh, we started out believing we were in love and the fates were against us with Olivia tied in the way she was, but as the years passed and neither of us ever really tried to change the arrangement I think we both realised we had just been using each other as emotional props—Olivia because of the way her marriage was, me because I basically just didn't have the time or need for an emotional entanglement that would demand too much from me at a time when my career was of paramount importance to me. Not that it isn't now,' he grimaced. 'But then I was trying to establish myself. It wouldn't have been fair to any woman to offer the life I could have given her then—the days and nights of loneliness—whereas Olivia was part of that career, understood the demands; the two of us offered each other sympathy and support rather than anything else!'

Helen shook her head disbelievingly. 'I've seen the two of you together, the deep respect and love——'

'Of colleagues,' Zack cut in impatiently. 'It was never really more than that. Helen, Olivia's husband died a year ago—— That's right,' he confirmed as she gasped. 'It made absolutely no difference to our relationship.'

'Because *you're* now married to me!' Helen wailed.

'A marriage I have told you I'm in no hurry to end,' he pointed out grimly. 'I don't love Olivia, Helen, not in a romantic way. And she doesn't love me either. We have a brotherly-sisterly affection for each other.'

'But——'

'And she liked you very much, approves of the way you stand up to me.' His mouth twisted wryly. 'Helen, Olivia met someone she could love a few months ago; they're getting married next month. I'm going to be one of their witnesses.'

Helen searched the darkly hewn beauty of his face for some sign of regret at having lost the other woman to someone else after all these years.

'You won't find any,' he ruefully guessed her thoughts, smiling gently. 'Would you like to know when I really knew that what I felt for Olivia had never been the kind of love that binds a man and woman together for a lifetime?'

Her breathing felt constricted in her throat, and she moistened her lips with the tip of her tongue.

'It was the day I made love to the woman I *did* feel that kind of love for,' he told her huskily when she made no reply.

Helen swallowed hard, sure that she couldn't be mistaken about the emotion she saw in his eyes. And he was looking directly at *her*. 'Me?' she squeaked.

He nodded, sighing heavily. 'I did you a great wrong by marrying you in the way that I did, forcing a situation you so obviously didn't want, even using blackmail to achieve my own ends.' He shook his head. 'After we were married I very quickly came to realise all the reasons why my mother valued you so highly. And there was absolutely nothing I could do by this time to redeem myself in your eyes!'

Zack *loved* her. He really did love her, had loved her two years ago too!

He gave a low groan. 'I was full of self-disgust when I took advantage of the highly charged emotional situation after my mother died,' he rasped harshly. 'My God, you cried!' He sprang up from the sofa to pace the room. 'I'll never forget seeing you cry. The memory has haunted me for the last two years!'

'Zack!' Helen reached out a hand to him but he didn't seem to see her, lost in the misery of his self-recrimination.

He shook his head, his jaw tight. 'I love Emily dearly, always make her welcome, but every time she comes here it's gut-wrenching agony because she's so like you!'

'Emily is...?' she gasped. That beautiful, exotic creature she had always been slightly in awe of having given birth to?

Zack looked down at her with gentle reproach. 'You've never been able to see your own worth, Helen; it's the one thing I've wanted to shake you for!'

It was there, it was all there, in the dark, loving caress of his eyes, everything that she was, everything that she could be.

'But I'm going to, Zack.' She held his gaze as she slowly got to her feet. 'With you at my side I'm going to find out exactly what sort of person I am.' She stood in front of him now, his gaze uncertain on her upturned face. 'I cried that day because our lovemaking was so beautiful, Zack,' she told him huskily. 'And the next time we make love I will probably cry again, for exactly the same reason.'

A nerve pulsed in his cheek, but otherwise he was very still. 'Next time?' he repeated haltingly.

'Next time,' she nodded, gaining in confidence all the time, able to see the effect that her closeness was having on him, the love in his eyes for her. 'I love you, Zack,' she told him without hesitation.

'Oh, God, *Helen*!' he groaned as his arms came about her to crush her to him. 'I love you too, my darling. I love you so much! How long——?'

'Not long after we were married,' she smiled ruefully as she answered that question of all lovers. 'It didn't take me long to realise all the reasons why your mother valued you so highly too.' There were tears in her eyes, but they were tears of joy.

'Two years!' he agonised. 'What a damned waste of two years,' he murmured against the softness of her throat.

'Let's not waste any more time, Zack,' she agreed.

He slowly raised his head to look down at her, at the longing in her face. 'You've only just come out of hospital,' he reminded her

reluctantly, the flare of love in his eyes showing her that he wanted to make love to her as
much as she obviously wanted him to.

'We'll find a way, Zack.' She glowed up at
him.

His eyes were almost black as he swung her
up into his arms. 'I'll try to be gentle—but it
won't be easy,' he added with rueful self-
mockery.

'I told you we wouldn't need the whole
three months,' a voice murmured conspira-
torially from the doorway behind them.

'Just when I was becoming fond of this ring
too!' came the slightly disgruntled reply.

Helen turned sharply in Zack's arms to
look at her daughter and Greg as they stood
across the room, colour blazing in her cheeks
as she realised that they must have heard at
least some of the conversation—the most intimate part!

Greg strode confidently into the room,
slapping his father good-naturedly on the
back. 'It's about time you came to your senses
and realised what a mistake you were making
in letting Helen go!'

Zack looked at his son with narrowed eyes, maintaining his hold of Helen in his arms even though she wriggled to be put down. 'And just what did the two of you mean by those remarks you made a few seconds ago?' he prompted slowly.

Greg grinned unabashedly. 'Emily and I came up with a plan to get the two of you talking to each other again before you could go through with the divorce.' He shrugged at the obvious success of that plan.

'Your own engagement!' Helen gasped incredulously as Zack slowly lowered her to the carpeted floor; she was almost unable to believe that that could possibly have been the 'plan'—and yet that was when she and Zack had started talking again!

She stared at Emily accusingly, had never realised that her daughter was capable of such subterfuge.

'Oh, Mummy, we did it with the best intentions in mind.' Emily moved to briefly hug her. 'Only because we were sure the two of you really cared for each other, and that stubbornness was going to take you through the divorce without either of you ever admit-

ting how you felt. And it worked, didn't it?'
She gave a gleeful smile. 'You and Zack aren't
getting divorced after all, are you?' she said
happily.

'No, we aren't,' Zack drawled, his arm
firmly about Helen's waist as he held her to
his side. 'And the two of you aren't getting
married—are you?' he said knowingly.

Emily looked down wistfully at the diamond and emerald engagement ring on her
finger. 'It might be worth marrying him just
to keep this lovely ring!'

'Thanks!' Greg grimaced. 'But I don't particularly want to be married for a ring.'

'But I——'

'Why don't the two of you go away and ar-
gue about this somewhere else?' Zack suggested pointedly. 'Helen and I were in the
middle of an important—discussion, when
you interrupted,' he reminded them huskily.

'So you were.' Emily gave a rueful grin at
her and Greg's insensitivity now that they had
achieved what they set out to do, putting her
arm through the crook of her stepbrother's.
'Come along, *darling*,' she grinned at him

impudently. 'Let's go and discuss the engagement ring upstairs.'

Helen was still stunned by the whole conversation, couldn't believe—— 'They actually went through a mock engagement just to get the two of us together?' she said incredulously.

'"And it worked."' Zack wryly echoed Emily's words as he turned Helen into his arms, their bodies moulded together. 'Let's not worry about how it happened; we can talk to our offspring about that later. A lot later,' he added softly. 'For the moment let's just be grateful that we're finally together. And that we're staying together. I actually think,' he added with amusement, 'that their little plan might have backfired on them, anyway,' he murmured with indulgence.

Helen blinked up at him frowningly. 'Hm?'

Zack smiled down at her. 'The two of them *are* good together. They may not realise it yet, possibly not for some time, but I have a feeling they may very well be announcing their real engagement one day.'

Helen thought of the easy affection between the two, the camaraderie. But occasionally, such as on the night of Emily's party, she had seen a spark of something else too. Zack could be right; she had a feeling he probably was.

'I'm glad they decided to interfere in our lives this time,' Zack continued ruefully. 'But it isn't something I want them to make a habit of, especially if they decide to gang up on us for good one day! But I've just thought of a wonderful way we could teach them a lesson for their intervention this time,' he said softly.

Her arms became entwined behind his head as she gazed up at him. 'And what's that?'

'We could always give them a little brother or sister they have to baby-sit for!'

A child. Between Zack and her. 'Oh, yes, Zack.' Helen glowed up at him at the mere idea of carrying his child. 'Yes, please.'

He laughed throatily as he swung her back up into his arms, taking determined strides towards the door.

'Zack,' she voiced tentatively. 'Last Saturday, when I stayed here because I was— ill; did we make love?' She frowned up at him.

He looked down at her with loving eyes. 'Did you cry?'

No, she was sure she hadn't, just as she was sure now that they hadn't made love. 'Then why——?'

'Even arguing with you is fun, Helen,' he told her indulgently.

It *was* exciting, made her feel truly alive. 'Take me upstairs and make me cry, Zack,' she invited breathlessly.

'Now there's a suggestion!' he lightly teased.

But he did.

And she did.

Ecstatically...

Share the adventure—and the romance—of

HARLEQUIN PRESENTS®

A Year
DOWN UNDER

If you missed any titles in this miniseries,
here's your chance to order them:

Harlequin Presents®—A Year Down Under

#11519	HEART OF THE OUTBACK by Emma Darcy	$2.89	❏
#11527	NO GENTLE SEDUCTION by Helen Bianchin	$2.89	❏
#11537	THE GOLDEN MASK by Robyn Donald	$2.89	❏
#11546	A DANGEROUS LOVER by Lindsay Armstrong	$2.89	❏
#11554	SECRET ADMIRER by Susan Napier	$2.89	❏
#11562	OUTBACK MAN by Miranda Lee	$2.99	❏
#11570	NO RISKS, NO PRIZES by Emma Darcy	$2.99	❏
#11577	THE STONE PRINCESS by Robyn Donald	$2.99	❏
#11586	AND THEN CAME MORNING by Daphne Clair	$2.99	❏
#11595	WINTER OF DREAMS by Susan Napier	$2.99	❏
#11601	RELUCTANT CAPTIVE by Helen Bianchin	$2.99	❏
#11611	SUCH DARK MAGIC by Robyn Donald	$2.99	❏

(limited quantities available on certain titles)

TOTAL AMOUNT	$
POSTAGE & HANDLING	$
($1.00 for one book, 50¢ for each additional)	
APPLICABLE TAXES*	$ _____
TOTAL PAYABLE	$ _____

(check or money order—please do not send cash)

To order, complete this form and send it, along with a check or money order for the
total above, payable to Harlequin Books, to: *In the U.S.*: 3010 Walden Avenue,
P.O. Box 9047, Buffalo, NY 14269-9047; *In Canada*: P.O. Box 613, Fort Erie, Ontario,
L2A 5X3.

Name: _____

Address: _____ City: _____

State/Prov.: _____ Zip/Postal Code: _____

*New York residents remit applicable sales taxes.
  Canadian residents remit applicable GST and provincial taxes.   YDUF

POSTCARDS FROM EUROPE

HARLEQUIN PRESENTS®

Hi!
Spending a year in Europe. You won't believe how great the men are! Will be visiting Greece, Italy, France and more.
Wish you were here—how about joining us in January?

There's a handsome Greek just waiting to meet you.

THE ALPHA MAN
by Kay Thorpe

Harlequin Presents #1619

Available in January wherever Harlequin books are sold.

HPPFEG

HARLEQUIN®

PRESENTS® *plus*

Meet Lily Norfolk. Not even her husband's tragic death can convince her to tell his brother, Dane Norfolk, the truth behind their marriage. It's better that he believe she married Daniel for his money and that she had an affair with Daniel's best friend. It's better that Dane keep his distance!

And then there's Elizabeth. She's a respectable young woman, but she also has a secret mission and a secret repressed sensual side. Jake Hawkwood's never liked secrets—he's determined to uncover everything Elizabeth's been hiding....

Lily and Elizabeth are just two of the passionate women you'll discover each month in Harlequin Presents Plus. And if you think they're passionate, wait until you meet Dane and Jake!

Watch for
HOUSE OF GLASS by Michelle Reid
Harlequin Presents Plus #1615
and

THE HAWK AND THE LAMB by Susan Napier
Harlequin Presents Plus #1616

Harlequin Presents Plus
The best has just gotten better!

Available in January wherever Harlequin Books are sold.

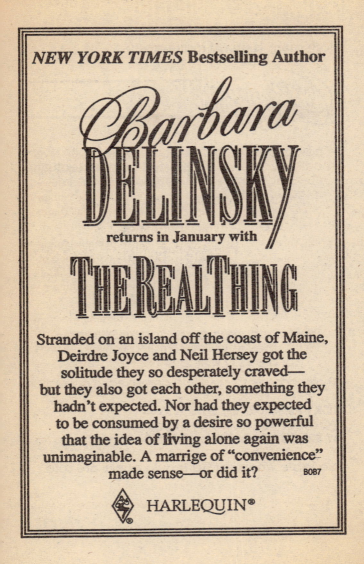

NEW YORK TIMES Bestselling Author

Barbara DELINSKY

returns in January with

The Real Thing

Stranded on an island off the coast of Maine,
Deirdre Joyce and Neil Hersey got the
solitude they so desperately craved—
but they also got each other, something they
hadn't expected. Nor had they expected
to be consumed by a desire so powerful
that the idea of living alone again was
unimaginable. A marrige of "convenience"
made sense—or did it? B087

HARLEQUIN®

When the only time you have for yourself is...

Christmas is such a busy time—with shopping, decorating, writing cards, trimming trees, wrapping gifts....

When you do have a few *stolen moments* to call your own, treat yourself to a brand-new *short* novel. Relax with one of our Stocking Stuffers—or with all six!

Each STOLEN MOMENTS title
is a complete and original contemporary romance that's the perfect length for the busy woman of the nineties! Especially at Christmas...

And they make perfect **stocking stuffers**, too! (For your mother, grandmother, daughters, friends, co-workers, neighbors, aunts, cousins—all the other women in your life!)

Look for the STOLEN MOMENTS display in December

STOCKING STUFFERS:

HIS MISTRESS Carrie Alexander
DANIEL'S DECEPTION Marie DeWitt
SNOW ANGEL Isolde Evans
THE FAMILY MAN Danielle Kelly
THE LONE WOLF Ellen Rogers
MONTANA CHRISTMAS Lynn Russell

HSM2

 WORLDWIDE LIBRARY

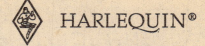 **HARLEQUIN®**

If you enjoyed this book by

CAROLE MORTIMER

Here's your chance to order more stories by one of
Harlequin's favorite authors:

Harlequin Presents®

#11451	MEMORIES OF THE PAST	$2.89	☐
#11468	ROMANCE OF A LIFETIME	$2.89	☐
#11543	SAVING GRACE	$2.89	☐
#11559	THE JILTED BRIDEGROOM	$2.99	☐
#11583	PRIVATE LIVES	$2.99	☐

(limited quantities available on certain titles)

TOTAL AMOUNT	$
POSTAGE & HANDLING	$
($1.00 for one book, 50¢ for each additional)	
APPLICABLE TAXES*	$ _____
TOTAL PAYABLE	$ _____
(check or money order—please do not send cash)	

To order, complete this form and send it, along with a check or money order for the
total above, payable to Harlequin Books, to: *In the U.S.*: 3010 Walden Avenue,
P.O. Box 9047, Buffalo, NY 14269-9047; *In Canada*: P.O. Box 613, Fort Erie, Ontario,
L2A 5X3.

Name: _____

Address: _____ City: _____

State/Prov.: _____ Zip/Postal Code: _____

*New York residents remit applicable sales taxes.
  Canadian residents remit applicable GST and provincial taxes.

HCMBACK1